THE ROGUE REGIMENT

THE ROGUE REGIMENT

PIXIE REBELS™ BOOK ONE

MARTHA CARR
MICHAEL ANDERLE

This book is a work of fiction. All of the characters, organizations, and events portrayed in this novel are either products of the author's imagination or are used fictitiously. Sometimes both.

Copyright © 2023 LMBPN Publishing
Cover by www.mihaelavoicu.com
Cover copyright © LMBPN Publishing
A Michael Anderle Production

LMBPN Publishing supports the right to free expression and the value of copyright. The purpose of copyright is to encourage writers and artists to produce the creative works that enrich our culture.

The distribution of this book without permission is a theft of the author's intellectual property. If you would like permission to use material from the book (other than for review purposes), please contact support@lmbpn.com. Thank you for your support of the author's rights.

LMBPN Publishing
PMB 196, 2540 South Maryland Pkwy
Las Vegas, NV 89109

Version 1.00, February 2023
ebook ISBN: 979-8-88541-954-3
Print ISBN: 979-8-88878-121-0

THE ROGUE REGIMENT TEAM

Thanks to our Beta Readers
Larry Omans, David Laughlin, Malyssa Brannon, Rachel Beckford

Thanks to our JIT Readers

Dorothy Lloyd
Peter Manis
Jackey Hankard-Brodie
Diane L. Smith
Wendy L Bonell
Christopher Gilliard
Daryl McDaniel
Dave Hicks
Jan Hunnicutt

CHAPTER ONE

The Key Bank was as dark and empty and securely shut down for the night as every other building at 11:27 p.m. in Salt Lake City, Utah.

Just not securely enough.

If anyone had bothered to take a closer look, they would have seen flickering lights inside the bank lobby that didn't look like the normal blinking lights from security cameras and silent alarm systems. They would have seen a miniature flash of movement here, a tiny streak of color there, and the doors to the cash and safe deposit vaults slowly opening on their own.

They wouldn't have been able to make sense of what they saw happening inside this Key Bank branch. It would have looked like fireflies were pulling money out of everywhere close to midnight when everyone else was safely tucked in bed.

This was just another night for the roving gang of pixies that was pulling off one hell of a bank heist. A well-trained gang of pixies, actually, led by Calinda who had handpicked every one of them for a particular skill set. Back on Oriceran, they had a rep and the gruesome Trevilsom prison had been mentioned more than once, but here it was a different story.

"How's the security system looking, Marv?"

"A freakin' joke, just like the last one."

"Bill! I'm finally gonna get that Barbie car. You know the one, the hot Corvette! Look at all these bags they left us. I feel like I owe them a thank you note."

"You know you can fly anywhere, right? Tiny wings on your back?"

"Yeah, but it's nice to have choices."

"What're you waiting for, Kilder? Use the bags and fill 'em up."

"Hell, yeah!"

"Hasher, what did I tell you about tagging the walls like that when we're on a job?" yelled Calinda. *Small can be beautiful* was spray painted in neon orange on the wall.

"Aw, come on, Calinda. I was just—"

"What did I say?"

"I'm leaving clues behind, but how does that give us away? Nobody here will think, magic. They'll think vertically challenged thieves."

"Quit tagging the walls and get back to work. We don't have a lot of time."

"Sure, sure, no problem." Hasher added a spray-painted ant, his tag, and flapped his wings, zipping back to the teller drawers. Calinda rolled her eyes but was smiling at the same time.

"Remember, we got into this to also have fun," said Kilder, still stuffing a bag with twenty dollar bills big enough for him to use as a bath towel.

"It's fun till they catch us. Okay, everybody, hurry up. Ten minutes to take whatever you want and trash the rest. Then we're outta here."

A cash drawer at one of the teller windows pinged open, and a lime-green flash of light darted down from the ceiling and hit the open drawer with a jingle. A squeaking grunt of frustration rose from the pixie behind the counter. "Seriously? I finally get the thing open, and all they put in here are rubber bands and paperclips!"

"I could use some of those to make a hammock. Save me some, will you?" asked Hasher, his wings beating so fast they looked like a blur of glowing blue. "Bill, you help me?"

"The bank's closed, Syd. They keep all the money over there by the... Well, look at that. Vernon got into the tellers' cash safe."

"Guys. Hey, guys!" Loose bills shot up from the open safe under the drive-through teller window, then fluttered all over the place in a rain of rustling green. "Look, it's snowing!"

"That can be *your* cut, Vernon."

"What? This is my idea of fun."

"Whatever you want, man. It's *your* cut."

"Has anyone seen the triplets?"

Snorts and high-pitched snickers filled the bank's lobby.

"I saw 'em headed for the safe deposit vault. They're probably Scrooge McDuckin' another crazy pile like last time." Vernon did a backstroke, floating a foot across the lobby, kicking his small feet.

"Yeah, they're good at that, aren't they? Let's get a move on, pixies. We don't have all—" The pixies' laughter echoed across the lobby. "What am I saying? Of course, we have all night! There's nobody here!"

The pixies flittered back and forth across the lobby and behind the teller windows laughing and falling all over each other, shoving cash into bags at the same time. Fun is fun, but they were well trained. In the end, the mission came first.

Three of the pixies in Calinda's gang—affectionately nicknamed "the triplets" by the others—were too far away to have heard everyone laughing in the front of the bank. It was hard for Z Thornbrook to hear much of anything beyond the click and scrape of the cylinder in the lock housing, moving with agonizing slowness as she pushed it with both hands—from inside the lock. Dark tattoos of different numbers, one per finger, stood out against her pale skin. Speculation in the group was that the numbers were a combination to something valuable on Oriceran. But Z wasn't the type to share information and her ability to throw a punch or a magic spell at the slightest provocation was very well known. She would tell them when she was ready, or never.

A murmur of laughter reached them, and Z's pointed ears twitched, taking it in.

"They sound like they're wasted," her cousin Domino muttered. "Think we should wrap it up pretty soon?"

Z grunted and doubled down on her efforts to push the

mechanism's tiny pieces into place without the key. "After I get this one open. I have a real good feeling about what's in here."

Domino positioned himself in front of the vault's single long table, and didn't flinch when a box beside Z popped open with a metallic clang. A flash of beating wings the color of dull steel darted out of the box, zipped over, and stopped beside Domino with a soft pop.

A grey pixie was quickly growing to the size of a small seventh grader, crowing Domino. He was used to it. "I got this, Echo," said Domino. He was the quiet elf's brother and protector. The two of them were part of the pixie clan from the mountains of Oriceran. They were known for their ability to get in and out of tight, tiny crevices and then grow large enough to push rocks out of the way.

Echo had landed perfectly, appearing next to her brother in front of the table, towering over him. She was dressed in black fishnets, knee-high combat boots, and a tank top with dozens of rips across the back. Just how she liked it. Echo was the quiet one amongst them, with a lot going on inside. Everyone in the gang knew not to underestimate her.

The added size was needed occasionally for bigger jobs when a pixie's natural tiny stature wouldn't cut it. "Trolls have got nothing on us," Domino trumpeted, flying around his sister in a quick circle.

As she folded her glittering black wings against her back, Echo leaned toward her younger brother. Her straight black hair fell over half her face like a thick curtain, framing a thin scar that ran down the side of her nose. No one ever asked about it. Domino made sure of that and besides, Echo would not have answered.

She tucked a lock of hair behind her ear and whispered in Domino's small ear.

Domino relayed, "She says, that's what you said about the last three boxes. On the last three jobs."

"Even a larger size, she won't say something directly to me," muttered Z, shaking her head. "Well, Echo, you're not *wrong*." Sighing, Z double-checked how far she had left to push. "And technically, I didn't *not* find really good stuff inside all of them."

Domino snorted and folded his arms, his golden-brown wings twitching against his back. "At this point, I honestly care more about getting out of here before Bill and Hasher start another contest to see how far they can throw each other. Still not sure why you're into all this money. I mean, we're magicals," he said, holding his arms out wide.

"It's kind of like a language thing. If you want to trade with humans, you have to speak their language, and money talks," Z retorted with another grunt of effort. "Be grateful this stuff is still protected by vaults and alarms. I mean, me, I keep the important stuff inside an enchanted drawer or a tree stump with a few trolls I can slip some elderberry honey. That's their love language."

"Oh, *right*. Instead of a bank without wards or protective spells, so any magical can break right in and take whatever they want."

Z leaned sideways against the cylinder and smirked. "Not just any magical, Dom. *Us*."

Echo leaned toward her brother again to whisper in his ear.

Domino playfully rolled his eyes. "She says if *you* don't use magic to open that lock, *she* will."

"That's not the point and it could alert the Silver Griffins. Then we would have a problem."

"She says you're wasting—"

"Yeah, yeah. I get it." Z pushed away from the cylinder and stood up inside the lock, glaring at the mechanism that shouldn't have been so difficult to push into place. She flicked her finger at it.

A bolt of bright blue light burst from her fingertip and clanged against the metal cylinder. "Silver Griffins be damned," she muttered. The last millimeter of metal slid into place the way she wanted, and the deposit box's lid sprang open. Z looked through the keyhole at her human-sized cousins, giants compared to their natural pixie dimensions. "I pushed it most of the way there."

"Uh-huh. What was that?" Domino looked at his wrist and the nonexistent watch on it. "A whole five minutes? Woohoo!"

"Hey, I'm trying to be a little more disciplined." Z jumped off the box, and her shimmering blue wings, the same hue as her short hair, carried her up and over the table toward her cousins. With a soft pop, she grew to human size as well, standing on the other side of the still snack-size Domino.

All three pixies stared at the open box.

Echo studied Z for several seconds before whispering in her brother's ear again.

Domino snickered. "She says forget five minutes. Do you have any idea what a zap could've done in five *seconds?*" He was floating between the two, glancing back and forth.

Z's ears twitched and she stared at his sister. "We're the only ones in here, Echo. You don't have to keep—"

"Yeah, but the others could walk in here at any second," Domino interrupted. "She's not gonna talk."

Z glanced at the open door of the vault and shrugged. "I *do* know what a fun little zap can do, by the way. I'm just trying to spice things up. You know, add a challenge every once in a while."

Her cousins choked back their laughter with poorly muffled snorts.

"This is why our family reunions turn into food fights." It was true. Hundreds of pixies trying to pull a fast one, always making a joke. It was only a matter of time before someone threw a plump blueberry at somebody else. It always ended in a family picture, tiny arms around each other, decorated in tomato sauce and saffron.

She fixed them with a deadpan stare. "You think that's funny."

"Grand theft isn't a challenge to you? You don't need a challenge, Z." Domino's voice trembled in his attempt not to laugh at her. "You need a life."

"I *have* a life. I spend it keeping *you* two ingrates alive and out of Trevilsom."

Echo whispered in her brother's ear, and he nodded vigorously in agreement. "She says you need a hobby, so add that to the list. Or a date. I added that one."

"Oh, yeah. Thanks. Screw you too," Z snickered. Her cousins laughed harder, Domino landing on Echo's shoulder. Z nodded at the deposit box Echo had opened. "Find something useful in that, huh? Domino, you doing another one?"

"Nah." With a grimace of distaste, he adjusted his hands on the large duffel bag he'd been holding open for the women the whole time. "I like it right here where it's easy to see everything. You don't want me crawling into any more locks anyway. I'd just end up showing you how it's *really* done."

"Uh-huh. Keep talking." Shaking her head, Z rubbed her hands together over the safe deposit box, fingers twitching. "Gimme something good."

She pulled the lid of the box back and let it ping against the table, disappointment instantly washing over her. "Another watch? Seriously?"

"Think it's real?" Domino asked.

"That's not my area of expertise, dude. I don't know, somebody bothered to put it in here."

"Well, toss it in the bag. If it's junk, *I'll* wear it."

The jingling and clinking of gemstones and metal filled the vault as Echo pulled a gaudy necklace dripping with diamonds and rubies from her box. She shook the heavy piece of jewelry and grinned.

Domino barked a laugh. "Sure hope *those* are real."

Echo tossed the fabulously valuable necklace into the duffel bag with everything else they'd scored in this room. Z tossed the possibly fake Rolex over her shoulder, and Domino jerked the duffel bag forward to catch it.

"Personal documents," Z muttered, pulling papers out of the box and tossing them across the table in a scattered mess. "More personal documents. This guy must think he's the King of the Earth?"

Domino cleared his throat. "Echo says there's no such thing—"

"It's a figure of speech."

The siblings shared a confused look, then Domino wrinkled his nose. "Says who?"

She ignored her cousin and kept rifling through the box. Passports. Credit cards. Wads of cash in four foreign currencies.

Might be useful. Weird. This looks like the kinda box that'd have a stupid gun at the bottom, and that's the last thing we need to have around Hasher or Bill. Wait, what?

Z froze with a passport in her hand and stared at the last item in the box. It wasn't a gun.

What in the world is some man with fake names and plenty of cash doing with Oriceran symbols on a shady looking package hidden at the bottom of his safe deposit box? And where have I seen this one before? Z tapped the top of a squiggle that ended in an 'o'.

The package at the bottom of the box was a little bigger than a standard mailing envelope. Judging by the way it bulged around the middle and pulled at the corners, it was stuffed full of *something*.

"Something far more important was locked up with the rest of its owner's mostly useless junk," muttered Z. She looked up at Domino, excited and calm. It's what always happened to her when a job took an unexpected turn. "It has to be magical since, as a general rule, humans didn't go around stamping Oriceran symbols on their paperwork."

"What is it? Finally find something good?" Domino asked, amused. "Can I get a look?" Domino was the one who was good with puzzles, including symbols. It was why

Calinda picked him. He flew around the box, trying to get a better look, the bag still clutched in his hand.

"Maybe." Tilting her head, Z studied the package. She didn't want to risk touching a potentially magical envelope and setting off a spell. "Whoever this guy is, he's got—"

"Hey, Triplets!" A sharp smack came from the open vault door. Riverly was standing there with a crooked smile, her hand on the door. "Wrap it up. Boss says it's time to move."

"Yep." Domino slung the stuffed duffel bag onto the table, pushing aside several deposit boxes they'd looted. Two slid off the table and crashed to the carpeted floor, scattering the contents. "That one's on me." He tugged the zipper shut with one swift movement and threw the bag's strap over his shoulder.

"Leave it," said Riverly. "There's no time."

Echo whispered in her brother's ear again.

He leaned away from her to fix her with a dubious frown. "Yeah, I *know* it's night, but nobody says, 'All in a night's work.' Or do they? Z, you have any idea?"

"I don't know. Elves? Are they real?" With the clock ticking, Z snatched the package stamped with Oriceran symbols, grinning when it didn't give off magical vibes. That didn't mean there wasn't any magic there, but at least it didn't blast her across the room because she touched it. She stuffed the package into the side pocket of her bomber jacket and spun toward the door. "Let's go."

She hurried out of the vault first, followed by Domino with the bulging, jingling duffel bag slung over his shoulder.

Last to leave the vault was Echo. She eyed the mess

they'd made of the vault. She smacked her hand on the table, the fallen pieces of paper and jewelry dancing in the air till they settled, forming a neat pyramid. "There," she whispered. Her own style of tagging.

The grey pixie walked out after the rest of her family with a smirk.

CHAPTER TWO

Z and her cousins rejoined the rest of Calinda's gang in the lobby of the bank.

"All right, you know the drill," Calinda called as she scanned the pixies forming a circle with her. Echo and Z still taller than the rest. "Everybody in."

"Hell of a haul."

"Can't wait to lay all this out on the table and roll around in it."

"Just don't break the table," said Z.

"Easy for *you* to say. You're the size of a healthy dwarf."

"I'm gonna choose to take that as a compliment." Z shrunk back down to pixie size, Echo following suit.

The lobby echoed with the laughter of a dozen satisfied pixies as they tossed their zipped, tied, twisted, and stacked loot into a chaotic pile in the center of the circle.

The last item to crash on cash-filled bags was a cash drawer ripped from its bolted slot at a teller window. Calinda glanced at the pixie who'd tossed it in. "Bill, not again. We've talked about this. You can't take pieces of the buildings."

"Aye aye, Cap'n." With hair so light and fine it was almost clear and eyelashes, eyebrows, and wings to match, Bill looked ridiculous when he gave their ringleader a sloppy salute.

Calinda raised one fuchsia eyebrow. "What were you planning to do with a cash drawer?"

He shrugged and let out a noncommittal hum before wiggling a pinky in his ear. "A home away from home. Make a little nest. Something like that."

"A few good rains and that thing will rust," Hasher cut in with a giggle.

"Hey, *you* don't know that. I could insulate it." Bill could build anything and had gotten them out of more than one scrape. Calinda picked him for the team after she caught him stealing silver hoop earrings from a willen, not an easy task, and followed him to find the home gym he was creating.

The other pixies laughed, and Calinda adopted a knowing but bemused smile, then she shrugged too. "Sounds good to me. Time to go. Fire it up."

They were the right distance apart, so every pixie settled their left hand on the shoulder of the magical on their left. When Domino's hand came down on Z's shoulder and gave it a playful squeeze, she shot him a sidelong glance and a crooked smile.

Like this is the most exciting part of what we do. Please. It's not even close.

Calinda led the gang by pointing her right hand at their huge pile of loot. Everyone else did the same.

The air crackled and popped with the sudden flare of combined, powerful magical energy. Z smiled at the intensity of the tingling buzz that raced over her body. She bit her lip to hide how much she enjoyed the sensation.

Lurch let out an unabashed giggle. Grulo barked a laugh, then pretended to look embarrassed that anyone else had heard it. Hasher's face was flush from the connection to the others.

Even Calinda was grinning at the swirl of euphoric energy racing from pixie to pixie in a continuous circle of superpowered magic few of their kind ever got to experience. Even fewer could create it on demand.

From the other side of Domino, Echo whispered in her brother's ear. He snickered, then relayed her comment to the rest, who were used to the way the siblings worked. "She says this is even better than Bird's peach-flavored moonshine."

Everyone cracked up, though no one removed their hand from their neighbor's shoulder or stopped pointing at the pile.

"Rock 'n roll, my pixies," Calinda murmured through a hazy, drunken-looking smile.

Those were the magic words.

Each pixie funneled the buzzing, humming energy they'd created into their hands and back out. Streams of light in varying colors and levels of brightness burst from a dozen fingertips.

The combined light grew so brilliant that the bank lobby filled with its blinding brightness. Then it winked out.

Outside in the parking lot, a homeless man shuffled by,

pushing a rickety shopping cart from Harmons, decorated with a faded blue bandana tied at the front, marking his property. It was impossible for him not to notice the blinding flash of light that flared to life inside, and he stopped to watch the show with awestruck eyes.

After the light disappeared he blinked as if he were coming out of a daze, shook his head, then shuffled onward in his nightly route around the city. "Nah, can't be. Got to stop eating out of the Taco Bell dumpster. First, a large, furry kewpie doll with green hair starts talking to me, and now this. Of course, he shared a donut. That was real. That's a friend. Now, what was his name?"

Scratching his head, he rattled the cans nestled on the pile of his belongings in the shopping cart, proud to have savings that couldn't be touched by bankers, aliens, or pixies.

If he'd stopped to look closer in the bank, he would have seen a dozen tiny glowing lights of many colors forming a perfect circle on the bank lobby's floor. However, he had places to be, and no one else was walking down that street at 12:14 a.m in Salt Lake City.

Inside, Calinda lowered her hand from her neighbor's shoulder, still grinning. "Whew. Gets me every time."

The other pixies let go as well. Some kept their eyes closed as the buzz and pixie-induced high faded. All were smiling.

Z's eyelids fluttered, and she gave a drowsy, contented sigh. "Good times."

"All right, fun part's over," Calinda called out. The pile of loot in the center of the circle had shrunk to pixie size.

"Well, the *funnest* part," she said with a wink. "Let's complete the mission."

"That's not a word, and I still love it." Marv laughed as he stepped forward to grab whatever bags he could get his hands on.

"Funnest part of doing what we do," Bill added, stooping to pick up the bulky cash drawer. "My new apartment," he said, trying to hug it.

"That's very sad, dude," said Hasher.

One by one, they picked up the loot and when the magically reduced pile had been strapped over shoulders and backs, Calinda pointed at the ceiling where it intersected with the side wall of the lobby.

Everyone knew what she meant. The buzzing hum of a dozen pairs of fluttering wings filled the air as every pixie launched off the lobby floor in a glowing ball of colored light. Letting out a high-pitched whistle, the pixie gang sped toward the air vent their ringleader had pointed at, racing each other and bobbing.

Z couldn't stop hiccupping. She was still intoxicated by the intense magic they'd used to shrink their haul. Even with the glowing lights of her fellow winged thieves zipping in spirals and curlicues around her, it was a straight shot to the vents.

Just as they'd planned, as if pixies ever followed a plan in a straight line. It's what made it so hard to catch them. There was a plan, but only a pixie would be able to see it.

When they were through the air vent and racing down the square metal tunnel behind it, the buzzing of their wings and high-pitched whistling were magnified.

The only sound that didn't belong was the hard metallic

clink Z heard as she followed her cousins. She stopped and looked down to see Bill's cash drawer lying on the floor of the vent. Bill hovered above her, flexing his hands. "That sucker is still awkward to carry."

Rolling her eyes, Z waited for the last few pixies to race past with their hauls before she dove toward the cash drawer. It wasn't as heavy as she'd expected it to be, even at its current size. She picked it up and clutched it against her chest, then took off after the others.

When Bill saw her, he stopped whistling and dove toward the glowing blue pixie carrying his new metal nest. "Hey."

"Hey." She fixed him with a lazy smile.

"That's mine."

"You dropped it."

Bill's face scrunched in a mixture of magical intoxication, confusion, and irritation. "It's not finder's keepers, Z. Get your own." He grabbed the cash drawer with both hands and yanked it from her arms.

Z slowed and glared at the back of Bill's red glowing wings. That was uncalled for.

"Fine," she hollered after him, picking up the pace. When she caught up with him, she waited for Bill to notice she was grinning like a lunatic. His eyes widened, just as she shoved him aside and raced ahead. "Keep it!"

Bill tumbled and hit the side wall with a muffled clang, still smiling. It always took a while for the magical surge to wear off. Till then, pixie mischief only rose.

The other pixies looked back. He was dizzily fluttering to the bottom of the vent. The last few pixies giggled, lazily bobbing their heads.

"Bill, that was Z 101 after a heist! You got schooled."

"After all this time, you still don't know how Z works, huh?"

"Give her the finger, and she'll give you the whole damn fist!"

When he'd recovered enough to understand what had happened, Bill shook his head and giggled as he clutched the cash drawer to his chest. Then he went airborne again to race after the others.

Z flew backward to make sure he saw he was still okay. "You should know better," she said, the typical edge to her voice. Bill chose that moment to flip her the bird, and she raised a fist in warning.

He dove to skim the bottom of the air vent so he could put the other pixies between them.

Humming a long-forgotten tune to herself that always calmed her down, Z caught up with her cousins and flew alongside them as the gang burst out from the other end of the air vent. They filled the night sky with colorful lights. Whooping and cheering, Calinda's gang flew loop-the-loops, spirals, and zigzags in celebration, still half-drunk on the magic they'd used to pull off their latest job without ever triggering the bank's security alarms. "Pixie's rule!" yelled Hasher, whistling.

CHAPTER THREE

Miles away in the woods at the foot of Utah's Mount Wire, Calinda's gang returned to their temporary hideout. Still whooping and shouting, the colorful point of light dove into a rotting log located half a mile off a walking trail. Half the log was open to the elements and the fresh air. The other half was enclosed by decaying wood that would maintain its structure for another month, assuming nobody stepped on it during an impromptu venture off the trail.

Some magicals would have worried about that plausible threat to their home. Calinda's gang, however, had been roaming across the country for the last hundred and fifty years, hopping from one temporary landing pad to the next out of necessity. No other magicals dared to pull off the kind of heists these pixies took on and then stuck around the area. That's why they kept moving. Well, one of the reasons. It was another trait Calinda had spotted that made them a good fit. None of them liked to stay in the same place for very long.

They were all used to abandoning or destroying their previous homes before setting off to find new, fresh, and exciting places to settle down and cause havoc behind the scenes. Calinda had collected the band of Pixies because they were the outcasts and the misfits on Oriceran. Always in trouble somewhere.

But she could see something else. They had potential, if only someone would pay attention long enough and let go of their ideas about pixies in general, or fun for that matter.

This rotting log had been their home for just over three weeks, and like every other place they'd chosen to temporarily call home over the decades, the gang had turned it into a chaotic, eclectic, easily disassembled paradise full of bits and pieces from other places. Their idea of home. Or at least a temporary one, and more than any of them had ever known before they became a family.

The stealing was a way to get by, and get back at everyone who saw pixies as a nuisance or a bother, and especially the Rogue Rebels. The nickname they had given each other a long time ago. Sure, it was safer to be on Earth than Oriceran, but magic was still hidden and what was a tiny creature with luminous wings to do? Money gave them a way to bargain with the pockets of humans who knew of their existence and would trade supplies or when a better hiding place was needed, or sometimes something fun. Like the time Bill traded his share of a job to get everyone a day to themselves at a carnival. No other humans, no other magicals around to give them sidelong glances.

Calinda smiled at the memory, looking at Z who was bent over her stash, carefully checking it to make sure nothing was missing. She was the toughest nut to crack in the Rogue Rebels. There wasn't anyone she trusted completely, and very few she trusted at all and they were all in the band of thieves. That was all Calinda knew of her story and she didn't ask for more.

That was a sure way to earn a scowl and maybe a jab or two from Z. "She'll tell me when she's ready, maybe," muttered Calinda. Honesty, or worse, vulnerability, wasn't a requirement of the group.

One after the other, the tiny magicals landed on their feet without a sound. Their glow faded when they touched down, and the pixies spread out on what they called "the front porch" to go through their loot and catalog everything. "What'd you find, Z" asked Lurch.

"Found," said Z, not looking up, or answering him.

Hasher grinned, pulling wrapped bundles of cash out of his bag. "Found," he said, nodding. "Pixie style."

Z and her cousins swooped toward the new couch they'd made. An empty upside-down sardine can that had been washed in the nearest stream served as the frame. Echo had stripped one black sock from her foot while she was human-sized to serve as its cushioned covering. A broken but still fluffy cattail pod tied to the can with dental floss was the backrest. It was the perfect size for the cousins, and fortunately, neither the sardine can, nor Echo's sock had stunk up the place. They were pixies after all. There were *some* standards. It's just that they were the only ones who knew them, but they were there.

The other pixies dropped their loot and headed to their favorite spot on the front porch: beds of leaves, cushions of moss, or hammocks made from scavenged medical gauze. Where natural materials or human trash didn't provide satisfying creature comforts, they had the odd bit of shrunken furniture like Calinda's crooked Papasan chair and Lurch's futon with mustard stains.

Z flopped onto the couch, put up her feet, and folded her arms behind her head with a contented sigh. "Home, sweet home."

Echo sat on the edge of the couch, her back straight and her hands resting on her thighs as she looked over her brother's shoulder. Domino sat on the floor on a fluffy layer of sawdust conveniently covering up a stretch of decaying wood. He put his back against the couch and their duffel bag between his outstretched legs.

The first thing he drew out of the bag was the gaudy necklace of diamonds and rubies. Lifting it on the end of one finger, he shook it, and looked happily around the porch. "Any takers on all this oversized icing? Echo, you like to be a full-size candy bar more than the rest of us." His sister silently shook her head, nudging it away, waiting for the next thing to be pulled out of the bag.

"'Icing?'" Hasher looked up from the cash he was counting. "You found a *cake* in the bank?"

"Could just be a tub of it," Riverly added without removing her gaze from the stacks of bills she had laid out in front of her. "But hey, if you found a tub of icing, I'd eat that shit all day long. Almost as good as Bird's peach-flavored moonshine."

The other pixies burst out laughing.

Bird held up two tiny gold bars, examining their shine in the warm glow of the enchanted lights bobbing above the porch. "How come everybody's comparing things to my hooch?"

"'Cause it's the best damn thing you've made since that farm in California."

"The pot farm? Ha! I didn't *make* that weed, Marv. I grew it."

"Wouldn't mind some of that now. It'd go real nice with a giant scoop of icing."

Echo whispered in her brother's ear.

"Shit." Domino jingled the necklace again. "My bad. I meant 'ice.' All this *ice*. That's what humans call crap like this, right?"

"Only if they're too cool to call it a diamond necklace," Z muttered.

"Huh." Bill stopped fiddling with his cash drawer and stared across the porch with a confused frown. "I thought they called it 'bing.' Like, 'Hey, man. Check out my *bing*!'"

Hasher and Lurch howled, falling against each other and kicking puffs of sawdust off the floor. "It's 'bling,' Bill. *Bling*!"

Bill shrugged and went back to organizing his snacks in their new home.

"How hard is it to get a straight answer?" Domino asked through his laughter. "Necklace with diamonds and rubies, if they're real. I don't have a jewelry guy, so if somebody else knows where to fence this thing, offer's on the table."

"I'll take it." Calinda held out a hand, and he nodded at

her before chucking the necklace across the porch. The finely crafted piece of jewelry lit up with a fuchsia glow and sailed into the ringleader's hand. Calinda undid the clasp and held the dangling necklace out in front of her. The gemstones sparkled in the enchanted lights suspended in mid-air above them. "You know what? I think these *are* real."

"Leave it to Calinda to find a jewelry guy after only a few weeks," Lurch muttered. He shook his head and chuckled.

"Oh, I haven't yet," Calinda replied casually. She studied the necklace with the same level of pride as if she'd crafted it herself, then laid the necklace against her chest and clasped it around her neck. "I think it completes my look."

The pixies roared at their leader. She was sitting cross-legged in the lopsided Papasan chair in a tattered jeans jacket, oversized sweatpants, fuzzy pink slippers almost the same color as her hair, and a bejeweled necklace that was probably worth more than the entire gang had stolen from every job combined. Reveling in the hilarity and attention, Calinda straightened like a queen looking at her subjects, then laughed along with them.

A moment later, Z dropped her head on the couch's back cushion and slid her hands into her jacket pockets. *It's like a bunch of kids at Christmas around here.*

She paused when her fingers brushed the bulky package she'd pilfered from the final security box. The Oriceran symbol stamped on the front of the package in crimson ink, without any other identifying marks on the envelope, flashed through her mind.

Weird to find something like that in a bank, of all

places. What would a human have to do with the kind of magic that gets stamped on an envelope?

Z started to pull the package out of her pocket, only half-listening to the jovial celebratory chatter of the pixies around her. The gang had become a family to her and her cousins. She stopped when a conversation caught her attention.

"Check this out, man!" Grulo shouted as he ripped open a bag to rummage through the contents. "Dammit, Marv. If you chucked a bunch of computer shit into one of our bags again, I swear to the Four Seasons I'm gonna—"

"Hey, isn't that a hotel? The Four Seasons?"

"What? No. That's the freaking weather on this planet, smartass."

"*Marv*," Calista cautioned, pretending to be perturbed. "We talked about stripping computer parts—"

"Hey, I quit computers cold turkey!" Marv spread his arms for everyone to see, having apparently forgotten that he was hooking up electronics to the porch swing he was building. The wires dangled from his hands, and when the rest of the gang stared at him, he gave their leader a sheepish smile and shrugged. "Okay, I still dabble from time to time, but I didn't touch a single computer in the bank tonight, boss. Honest."

"Then why are there blinking lights in a bag full of money?" Grulo asked, pausing while rooting around to find the source of the lights. "Huh?"

"It. Wasn't. Me."

"Let's have a look, then," Kilder shouted. "Show us whatcha got!"

"Yeah, yeah. Hold your pants on." Grulo sifted through

the bag a little longer, then mumbled, "Screw it," and upended it to send its contents toppling out onto the porch floor. Puffs of sawdust ballooned in all directions, most of it settling in Marv's thick, curly mop of indigo hair.

After flicking through the scattered stacks of cash, Grulo grimaced and flipped the duffel bag over to look inside. "I don't get it. Human money doesn't flash, does it?"

"Only if you've been drinking Bird's moonshine all night!"

"Yeah!" Bird leapt to her feet with a grin. "I'll go get it right now."

"Moonshine!" the others chanted, pumping their fists. "*Moonshine!*"

"Can you boneheads shut up for a second?" Grulo snarled. "I'm trying to figure out what—" He froze, staring at the inside flap of the duffel bag to one side of the zipper. "Uh-oh."

He didn't have to shout to grab everyone's attention. A pixie didn't say "uh-oh" like *that* unless it was really bad.

The laughter and good-natured ribbing came to a screeching halt. Even Bird stopped on her way to fetch a giant mason jar of her peach-flavored moonshine, which *hadn't* been shrunk like almost everything else. She turned to stare at the bearer of bad news.

Calinda gripped the curved sides of her Papasan chair and uncrossed her legs, then put her feet on the floor, sat up straight, and barked, "What is it?"

Baring his teeth in an apologetic grimace, Grulo remained silent but turned the plain black duffel bag inside out to reveal a small device affixed to its lining. It looked like one of those security tags clipped to expensive clothing in department stores, but this one had a black cover and blinked bright green.

"Lemme see that." Marv snatched the bag and took a closer look. "Aw, hell, Grulo. It's a damn tracking device."

The guilty pixie shook his head. "I didn't know."

The front porch filled with a cacophony of groans and grumbles as the pixies all voiced their complaints at once. Nobody cared that they couldn't hear themselves over the disappointed comments of their neighbors.

"I *knew* it was too good to be true!"

"Never, *ever* take an unmarked bag from a bank, man."

"Come on, Grulo. How dumb are you?"

"Dumb enough that if they'd hung a sign over the bag that said, Free bag. We'll use it to find you and ruin your life, he'd *still* take it."

"Now we have to move again."

"Dammit, I was starting to like this rickety old log."

Amidst the groans and whining and Grulo's protests and apologies, Z studied the woods. She hadn't *seen* anything out there, and she couldn't have heard anything from the woods over all the noise everyone else was making.

She sensed *something*, though.

It took her a few more seconds to figure out that, beneath the frustration and Grulo-shaming, she'd picked up emotions. That didn't make sense because Z normally didn't care about anyone else's feelings, with the exception of her cousins'. However, she wasn't making it up or blowing it out of proportion. She *was* feeling someone else's emotions and intentions, but she couldn't have explained what it was or why it was happening if she'd tried.

It had never happened before.

What was that? Hunger? No. Determination. Hunting? Frustration and pride and…closing in on a long chase?

She sat bolt upright, flung herself off the couch, and shouted, "Get rid of it!"

Everyone shut up and turned to her.

Bill snickered. "It's not a *bomb*, Z."

"No, it's a tracking device."

"Leading back to some security guard's computer that's probably shut off and is not even picking up a signal 'cause it's *the middle of the night*," Marv added and spread his arms. "Duh."

"We didn't trip any alarms," Calinda added. "There's no reason for anyone to check a tracking device now. Not until that bank opens in the morning and the humans find things slightly out of place."

The emotions Z had picked up on—the intentions coming from someone who wasn't her or the other pixies—were growing stronger and getting closer.

"It doesn't matter." She raised her voice to be heard over the commotion. "We don't have 'til morning."

"Oh, *right*." Hasher rolled his eyes. "It's all doom and gloom with you. Not a good look for you, Z."

"Naw, Echo called it!"

Laughter arose.

Domino and Echo fixed their younger cousin with questioning looks, and Z clenched her fists. "I said, get rid of it."

"Take a chill pill, Z," Bird suggested with a crooked

smile. She turned toward the back of the log when she remembered what she'd been doing. "Better yet, how 'bout a nice, long drink of—"

"Grulo!"

By the time he turned toward the couch to scowl at her for shouting his name, Z had launched toward him. She zipped across the front porch so fast that she left a trail of sawdust plumes in her wake and snatched the black bank bag out of his hand.

"Hey! What the—" Grulo whipped his head back as the blue-glowing pixie shot straight into the air with the shrunken bag dangling from her hand.

"Great." Calinda tossed her arms in the air, then swept a disapproving gaze across the gang. Only half of them noticed since the other half was leaning back to watch Z's flight. "Good job, everybody. Z just went nuclear."

"You mean psycho." Grulo gestured at the bobbing blue light, which was getting smaller and dimmer among the trees. "She took my bag."

"It's not *your* bag, dude," Domino cut in. Echo whispered in his ear, and he added, "She says you're the idiot who took it, though."

That got almost everybody laughing again.

Domino and Echo didn't share the others' amusement. Their close-knit group was falling all over each other and slapping thighs or the sawdust-covered floor or rolling on the piles of cash they'd stolen. The siblings shared a bland, unamused look.

"Any idea why she's freaking out *this* time?" Domino muttered.

Without expression, Echo glanced in the direction Z had disappeared and shook her head.

"Great. Guess we'll be on Z-cleanup duty again for the next couple—"

A bright blue streak shot down from the sky and landed in the center of the front porch with a thud and a puff of sawdust. The other pixies shouted and flinched in surprise. Lurch yelped and fell off his futon. No one noticed his mishap, and nobody laughed.

The orb of blue light in the center of the porch faded to reveal a scowling, pissed-off Z with her arms folded. She swept her gaze over the faces of the other pixies and settled her attention on Calinda.

The gang leader held Z's gaze and tilted her head in a mix of disapproval and reluctance.

Z had seen that look plenty of times, often directed at her, like right now. *She thinks I overreacted? Grulo's the idiot who brought a tracking device home with us, but she's not gonna do anything about it other than roll her eyes and laugh it off.*

Her gaze flicked toward her cousins, who were watching her with calm expressions.

No one else has anything they need to protect as much as I do. Not even Calinda.

With a snort, Z marched across the porch toward the curtain of soft leaves behind the couch and her cousins that led into the three-bedroom suite they'd hollowed out on the far side of the rotting log.

"Z!" Grulo shouted. "Where's my bag?"

"I got rid of it," she grumbled without stopping. "Like *you* should've."

"Dammit. You can't just take other pixies' stuff."

"You're welcome." Z strode past her cousins, shooting them a quick look which, after years of practice, they knew how to interpret. She was calling it a night.

She didn't get a chance to shove aside the leafy curtain or flop onto the comfortable bed of spongy moss she'd pulled off the outside of the log.

Calinda's gang had run out of time.

CHAPTER FOUR

A *click* rang through the woods and the gang's temporary home in the Utah mountains became flooded with a blinding white light so intense that it was hot.

Before anyone could figure out what it was, a voice boomed from the darkness of the underbrush no more than ten feet away, "We've got you surrounded. Come out slowly with your hands up."

For a second, the woods were silent save for the wind through the trees and the rustle of vegetation as a team of armed soldiers closed on the pixie gang's location. Most of the magicals burst out laughing. But Calinda was glancing around quickly, calculating what to do next. It was her job.

"Oh, come *on*," said Hasher.

"Seriously, who do these guys think they are?" asked Grulo. He was trying to pin a shiny button he found to his chest like a medal.

Calinda peeked out from the edge of the rotting log and could see the army fatigues and heavy, leather boots. "Military, not the police. What do they want with us?" She drew her head back in, her tiny arms cross over her chest and her wings beating furiously in frustration. "Vernon, did you do something I don't know about?"

"Wasn't me," he said, fluttering just above the ground, holding up his hands.

"They know we can dodge bullets, right? Please tell me they know."

"Hey, my pixie friend. Careful what you say out loud. I've heard about these guys," said Domino. "They don't like to get played."

"Awesome." Z tossed her hands up and shot her cousins an exasperated look. "That's all you guys like to do. This is not going to go well."

Bill shrugged and laid down on top of his bag, closing his eyes. Z looked over at Calinda, her jaw set. None of the others were paying much attention.

The soldiers marched closer to the log keeping their bright light trained on the gang.

"We have you surrounded. Come out with your hands behind your heads."

The Rogue Rebels laughed and let out a high-pitched whistle, a lot of them elbowing each other. It sounded like high-pitched squeaks to the highly trained squad tasked with hunting them down. The blinding beams of white light trembled as they moved back and forth along the rotting log. Some swung off into the woods behind the pixies' home, as the squad commander shouted again.

"I repeat, we have you surrounded. Come out with your hands behind your heads!"

Calinda zipped over to where Z was sitting, a trail of

light behind her. "This is bad. Soldiers tracked us. Hell, humans know about us. Somebody ratted us out, some magical."

"What do you want me to do about it?" Z gave her a cold look. She didn't like being cornered by anyone.

"This is your final warning," the soldier shouted through the trees. "You have ten seconds to show yourselves."

Calinda let out a deep sigh, then eyed the other pixies. They were counting on her to make the right call.

When Z saw the smile on her leader's lips, she felt herself relax. *She has an idea.*

"Hear that, pixies?" Calinda asked, standing up to her full two-inch height. "He wants us to *show ourselves*. Think we can do that?" Their leader cupped her hands around her mouth to bellow, "Don't shoot! We're coming out!"

Calinda put her hands on her hips and addressed her gang. "Operation Evade. We've done it hundreds of times."

"Okay if we have some fun while we do it?" asked Hasher.

"Why not? We're pixies, after all. It's kind of in our design." Calinda smiled. This wasn't the first angry group they had to get away from in the last century. It was just another day for them. "Let's go."

As if they shared one mind, the pixies launched into the air. Streams of multicolored light poured from the log's exposed cavity and arced into the air, coming down in all directions like a fireworks display.

A very dangerous fireworks display made up of clever pixies.

"Put your hands up!" barked the team leader.

A dark-red light zoomed toward the closest human. The soldier had his flashlight and the barrel of his gun still aimed at the log. To his surprise, Bill *popped* into human size two feet in front of his team leader. Both of Bill's hands were above his head and a loopy grin was on his face "Like this?"

The soldier swung his gun toward the pixie with red wings and fired two warning shots.

Bill was pixie-sized again in an instant. The shots barely missed the soldier's team leader. The red pixie saw his shot and swung a tiny fist into the side of the team leader's head and sent him reeling sideways. The man's eyes rolled back, and he dropped to the ground in front of his men. "Son of a bitch," swore a soldier, crouching to check on his commander. The rest of the squad were pointing their guns in different directions, trying to follow the zipping, colorful lights.

"No, Bill, he said *behind* our heads," Hasher shouted. He popped into human size in mid-air, legs splayed and arms folded behind his head. His wings kept him floating as if he were in an invisible hammock. He wiggled his eyebrows at the startled soldiers, then shrank and zipped off to bother somebody else.

"Fall back!" yelled one of the soldiers. "Fall back!" The pixies zipped faster, zigzagging through the group. The soldiers weren't sure where to pull back and avoid the pixies.

Sporadic bursts of semi-automatic weapons fire filled the woods. Bullets *thwacked* into tree branches and trunks and clumps of dirt. A surprising number missed the rotting log, but those that didn't took enormous chunks out of it. Each shot sent fragments of bark flying in all directions amidst plumes of sawdust and dirt and the personal belongings of the tiny twelve magicals who'd called that log their home.

"The porch!"

"Hey, you destroyed all our incriminating evidence!"

"Uh, Lurch, maybe leave that out of it?" Domino disappeared in a blur of color.

Whooping and whistling, the pixies dove toward the squad to deliver swift, powerful blows for such tiny creatures before zipping back into the dark sky. Some grew to five feet or a little more to taunt the men firing at them. Then they were off again in flashes of colored light.

The soldiers were scattered and unprepared to deal with zipping targets, but they'd been trained not to give up.

"You know, that has to count for something," Z said as she landed on the barrel of one man's automatic rifle. "You're dumb as shit, but you're still *trying* to do whatever it is you're doing."

It seemed as if the man hadn't heard her. He kept peering into the darkness of the woods, forcing himself to breathe steadily, with his rifle ready to open fire when he got a visual on a target.

"Determination," Z continued with a hefty dose of sarcasm. "If I didn't know better, I'd say *that's* the only thing keeping you humans alive. Even on your own planet. You just don't know when to quit."

The soldier scanned the woods a moment longer for the source of the high-pitched voice. When he realized it was coming from the glowing pixie standing on the barrel of his weapon with her hands on her hips, he yelped, still doing his best to hold his weapon steady.

Z barked a laugh. "Well, you get points for *that*. It's hard to surprise a pixie. Hey!"

She dove off the gun's barrel just before he smacked it like he was trying to swat a fly. The force of his hand moving through the air caused a shockwave that only someone as small as a pixie would notice. Z's wings fluttered furiously to keep her aloft. When she steadied herself, the man was slowly peeling his hand away from his weapon to check for splattered pixie.

White-hot rage flooded through her, and she darted toward his weapon with a furious growl.

The next thing he knew, his weapon was jerked out of his hands. He stumbled forward, stuttering in confusion, and swatted at his weapon in an attempt to seize it back.

"You wanna play it like that?" Z shouted. "Fine!"

He saw the scowling pixie holding his firearm by the very end of the barrel just before she cracked the stock against his skull.

The man crumpled into a limp, armored heap in the bushes, and Z tossed the weapon aside with a snort of disgust. "I'm not a bug you can squash, asshole."

She darted into the air to join the rest of the gang, which was wreaking havoc on the soldiers. Men shouted, and shots penetrated the woods to the sound of high-pitched, maniacal laughter. The soldiers dropped. Some were unconscious, and some groaned and nursed their injuries, but all were still breathing.

It looked like Calinda's gang had made short work of the giant, clunky humans who thought they could take them on, but Z saw someone else moving toward them. Even if she hadn't been able to feel the new upsurge of magic entering the small clearing around her home, she would have known the newcomer wasn't human.

Whoever it was hobbled through the bushes, hunched over, with an enormous stick in one crooked old hand keeping its wielder upright.

When the tip of that stick produced an electric-blue glow much lighter and brighter than Z's pixie magic, she knew they were in trouble.

She didn't have time to draw a full breath, let alone warn the others that another magical player had entered the game. The hunched figure jammed the end of his walking stick into the ground with a furious bellow and shouted, "That's enough!"

The blinding light burst from the tip of the stick and surged across the area in an explosive shockwave. The pixies couldn't avoid the blast; every one was frozen in place.

The blast surged across Z's body with a bitter cold that made her suck in a huge breath, and she couldn't move an inch.

No. I can breathe. I can blink. I can see.

Dazed by the magic used against them, the gang fell silent and floated slowly along their previous trajectories like pieces of junk moving through space.

They blinked at each other in surprise and incomprehension while the debilitated soldiers rolled around on the forest floor, gingerly touching heads, arms, legs, or groins or searching for their weapons.

Another set of blindingly bright lights switched on, these coming from the headlights of a vehicle. The magical who'd singlehandedly incapacitated a dozen pixies hobbled into that light, walking stick in hand.

CHAPTER FIVE

It's just a gnome flashed through Z's mind when the wrinkled old magical shuffled into the illumination. *How the hell did a* gnome *get magic like that? He's a dinosaur.*

Although she *could* open her mouth, she was too shocked to say anything.

Big surprise, the first pixie to break the silence was Bill.

"Hey! Hey, Pops! What gives, huh?"

The gnome turned a dark scowl on the him, then clasped his walking stick with both gnarled hands and leaned on it.

He didn't reply, which sent the rest of the gang into an uproar. If there was one thing pixies hated, it was being ignored.

"Let us go, you dumb old raisin!"

"When I can move again, the first thing I'm gonna do is take your stupid stick and set it on fire!"

"What did we ever do to *you?*"

"You're supposed to be on *our* side!"

"Cheat! You're a cheater! You cheated!"

"I thought gnomes were tiny and happy and fun."

That last comment got a burst of half-furious laughter from the gang, but the old gnome with the superpowered stick just glared at them.

Instead of shouting insults and demanding to be released from whatever this was, Z used the opportunity to call, "Domino? Echo?"

"I'd give you two thumbs-up, Z, but I can't feel my thumbs."

When her cousin responded, his voice sailed past behind her, but she couldn't turn to see if he was okay. He sounded fine.

"What about Echo?" she murmured now that she knew she didn't have to shout across the clearing filled with half-frozen floating pixies.

"Yeah, she'd give you a thumbs-up too. She's with me or a few inches away."

Z would have nodded, but when she tried, she couldn't move anything but her eyes and her mouth. She settled for, "Good. Any clue how to snap outta this?"

"Nope." Now Domino's voice came from her left, almost right beside her. "Gnome looks pissed, though."

When she gazed as far to the left as her frozen head would allow, all she could see was the scuffed toe of one of his sneakers.

The other pixies kept jeering at the old gnome, focusing on insulting him and his stick, but the magical just stood still among the groaning humans, presumably waiting for the noise to end.

"Look at him! Got in one hit, and he can't figure out what to do next!"

"What's the matter, Pops? Too scared to finish the job?"

"He looks like a one-shot kinda guy to me!"

"Or his old stick worked too hard and needs a nice long break!"

That got the whole gang laughing again, but when the grouchy old gnome thumped his walking stick on the ground and let off a warning flash, they shut up.

He looked them over, sweeping his beady gaze across the clearing in front of their destroyed home. "I'm only gonna say this once, and I'm hoping at least one of you has enough brains to give me the right answer. I'm here to talk to you. Forget the humans on the ground for now. They didn't know what they were up against, and the lot of you had your fun with 'em and then some."

One of the soldiers lying in a heap on the ground glared at the gnome and snorted derisively. The gnome had history with some of them, and the rest had heard the rumors.

The old magical ignored him and continued addressing the more pressing threat—the rogue pixies. "Will you give up long enough for us to chat before I get outta your hair?"

For a moment, the woods were silent. Then the pixie gang burst out laughing.

"You noticed we won this round, right?"

"Nice try, Pops. Come back when you have a *real* offer!"

Amidst the chaotic shouts and continued laughter, the gnome smacked his lips and let out a heavy sigh. "Yeah, that's what I thought."

"Even out the odds for us on this planet every day, gnome. Make it possible for us to live out in the open. Let us get back to just having fun. Can you do that?"

Marv buzzed around the gnome, tapping on his bald head.

"Marv, you have the best ideas!"

The old gnome rolled his eyes, unamused, then slammed the end of his walking stick on the ground once more with a thump. This time, he didn't bother with a warning. Another electric-blue pulse spewed from the tip and raced across every pixie who were now hanging frozen in the air.

Their taunts and laughter were cut off instantly, and the forest became much darker than it had been two seconds before.

Then, just like that twelve pixies and their glowing orbs were gone.

The gnome gave another heavy sigh, looking around at the soldiers still sprawled out across the forest floor. His wrinkled upper lip twitched in disdain as he scanned the unit that was supposed to have taken down the pixie gang. "Really? You're *still* on the ground? The whole thing was a joke from the start, but this is just pathetic."

They stopped groaning like a bunch of grandmas.

As the soldiers regained their bearings and their weapons and pushed to their feet, the man who'd snorted at the old gnome's attempt to parlay with the pixies brushed dirt and broken twigs off his uniform before scowling at the magical. "Nice trick. You couldn't've whipped it out and handled those little freaks *before* they turned on us?"

"Those pixies turned on you the second you started shooting up their home. Besides, I didn't want to miss watching you get your asses handed to you. You fellas needed a chance to feel like you'd accomplished something. Good job. I guess."

Staring at the vehicle still hidden in the trees, Carmine Ratchetter thumped his hickory walking stick on the ground again and clapped a hand on the pissed-off soldier's shoulder in a patronizing pat-pat.

As the old gnome hobbled toward the vehicle, every soldier stared after him with a mixture of confusion, disbelief, and disgust.

"I hate that goddamn gnome," one grumbled.

"Don't let *him* hear you say that."

Illuminated by the headlights, Carmine stopped three feet away and peered at the vehicle. To the men sitting inside, it seemed as if the gnome could see them through the blinding lights.

Sighing, Major Winters opened the rear driver-side door to step out of the vehicle.

"Major?" the driver said and started to unbuckle his seatbelt. "Are you sure—"

"Keep the engine running, Hornberg. This won't take long."

The young corporal nodded curtly, not looking any less worried, but he followed his superior's orders and tightened his grip on the steering wheel.

Major Winters left the rear door open and went over to the gnome while shooting glances at the unit of Special Forces soldiers picking themselves up off the forest floor.

When he arrived, Carmine stepped out of the vehicle's beams so he and Winters could have a face-to-face chat. "Told you it was gonna be a shitshow."

The officer who was in charge of the operation

grimaced and scratched his jaw. "You think they'll take the deal?"

"How the hell should *I* know?" Carmine snorted. "They're pixies."

"And you're the magical who agreed to consult with the US Army on this."

"Yeah, yeah. Keep your shirt on." The old gnome rolled his eyes and looked over his shoulder at the remains of the rotted log. "It ain't over yet."

Before Winters could say another word, Carmine smacked his staff on the ground and disappeared in a gnome-sized burst of light.

After the light faded and Major Winters could blink without seeing the gnome projected on the inside of his eyelids, the blue light and the crotchety gnome were gone.

Winters swallowed his frustration and turned his attention to the elite team of soldiers, who were mostly on their feet and had retrieved their weapons. "Pack up and move out. I have a meeting with a gang of goddamn pixies that I don't intend to be late to."

He started to turn back to his vehicle, then paused to fix the soldiers with a disappointed frown. "Judging by how that went down, we're better off calling 'em demons."

CHAPTER SIX

When Z's consciousness returned, it took her a moment to remember what had happened.

Humans with guns. Then the gnome. He froze us and said he just wanted to talk, then...

Her memories ended in blank black nothingness.

Why does everything hurt?

With a muffled groan, she moved as much as she could and felt cold, hard tile beneath her hands, forearms, and cheek. She slowly pushed up to sit in a daze, blinking heavily as her vision wavered between focused and multiple blurry images of whatever she was looking at.

Another groan escaped her as she gingerly touched her head. It felt like the stiffness and soreness from the rest of her body had traveled up to her temples.

"No," someone moaned from a few feet away. "What kinda cruel, fucked-up joke is *this*?"

Recognizing Grulo's voice, Z tried to turn to face him but was overwhelmed by a violent wave of dizziness that almost made her hurl.

"Tell me about it." Calinda's presence made Z feel better about being wherever they'd ended up. "And we didn't even *touch* the moonshine."

"Sorry, guys," Bird murmured, her voice stuffy and clogged up like she had a cold or a broken nose. "I'll be faster next time."

"Man, I'd give anything for a glass of your hooch," Marv added. "Then this wouldn't hurt so bad."

"*Why?*" Bill groaned, then curled up in the fetal position and stayed there.

"Nobody blames you, Bird." Lurch swallowed thickly, then let out a pained sigh. "By the way."

"Yeah, I know. Thanks anyway."

When Z felt like she could move without falling over or being sick, she scooted around to face the mystery room into which she and the other pixies had been rudely deposited. She only cared about two of them.

It was easier to find Echo since her goth cousin always wore the same colors, if not the same outfit. Black and more black. In a group of pixies where everyone had bright, colorful magic and personal style, Echo's outfits stood out like the grumpy gnome in the woods.

The pixie's black bob matched her black fishnets and cut-off jeans and the long-sleeved shirt that had been sliced to ribbons. She was on the opposite side of the strange room. The back of Echo's head rested against the white-painted concrete wall, and she had her arms folded and her eyes closed.

Z took a deep breath and let it out in a sigh of relief that made her only slightly dizzy. *She looks fine. That's good. Don't know if I can say the same about Domino until I find him.*

When it took her longer than a few seconds to find her other cousin, panic set in. If he'd been separated from her and Echo and been left behind, or worse, taken into custody and kept apart from his only real family, Z had failed.

It didn't matter that she was the youngest and angriest and most likely to blow things so far out of proportion that it had gotten them into even more trouble. Since the moment they'd left Oriceran and stepped foot on this planet, it had been her job to protect and look after her cousins. That was the promise she'd made to them and to herself after so many others had broken *their* promises. The rest of her family was...

Don't go there, Z. This isn't even close to that, and you know it. If Echo's still here, Domino can't be that far away.

She ignored the grumbling and whining and the occasional groan from the others and focused on finding him. When she looked at Echo again, the goth pixie's eyes were open, and her gaze was focused on Z. Instead of shouting across a room full of hurting, grouchy pixies who were either magically hungover or magically concussed, Z raised her eyebrows in a silent question.

Fortunately, Echo was one of those people with the uncanny ability to guess what someone was thinking just by looking at them. In her cousin's case, she'd had plenty of practice. Echo nodded, then turned her head and looked at the floor beside her. It didn't seem helpful until she met Z's gaze again and pointed at the same spot.

Leaning to the side to peer past the pixie bodies scattered around the twenty square feet of space in this room,

Z got a glimpse of the scuffed tip of Domino's sneaker beside his sister.

Jeez. Give me a heart attack, why doncha?

Despite her frustration, she shot Echo a reassuring smile. Her cousin didn't smile back, but when Echo rested her head against the wall and closed her eyes again, it meant the same thing.

Now what?

Feeling much better now that she knew her cousins were relatively safe, Z studied the room they'd woken up in.

Pixies were scattered across the white tile floor, yes, but the room had a long steel table and matching chairs that could have seated half of them. There were no windows, but there was an oversized mirror on the wall adjacent to where Echo and Domino had ended up. Across from that mirror was a plain white door with a brass knob.

That was it.

Frowning, Z couldn't put her finger on why everything looked strange. When it hit her, it was so simple that she almost laughed.

Shit. The old gnome made us the same size as humans and almost every other magical. Either that, or he's a creep who spends his free time making pixie-sized replicas of human rooms.

The thought made her snort, and Hasher gave her a confused grimace. "Must've hit your head too hard if you think this is funny."

Z shrugged. "The old guy *did* lock us all up in the same room. That makes me think he's scared."

"Of course he's scared," Calinda growled. "He stuck his nose in where it didn't belong and screwed with a pixie gang. If he's smart enough to stop us like that, he's smart enough to know he seriously fucked up."

Their leader's confident yet irritated pep talk put the other pixies in better spirits. Kilder tried climbing to his feet with his hands braced on the wall, then he swayed, shook his head, and plopped back down onto the floor.

"Hold on." Riverly frowned. "What do you mean he locked us up?"

"Yeah, you're right." Z folded her arms and gazed around the room. "This *could* be the gnome's version of a five-star resort."

"I *could* teach you a thing or two about being a smartass."

Deadpan, Z muttered, "Try it."

"You know," Grulo remarked, "this would be way easier to deal with if we didn't rip each other apart. Yeah?"

Riverly lost the staring contest with Z and dropped her gaze to her lap. "I just wanna know why she's saying we're locked up."

"It's obvious, Riverly." Calinda lifted a hand to her throat and laughed when she realized she was still wearing the necklace. "The real question is, what does that crooked old toad wanna talk about?"

"Yeah, and why's he working with those idiots?" Bill added, looking confused.

That wasn't a good enough answer for Riverly. "Nope. I'm not buying it." She pushed up off the floor with a grunt of frustration and a little leftover wooziness, then strode toward the door. Despite her efforts to walk in a straight line, she ended up stumbling like she *had* gotten into Bird's moonshine.

The gang's laughter at her antics was dampened by the headaches and nausea and dizziness none of them could control.

"Careful, Riverly. Don't want 'em to think you got your land legs back already!"

"Hey, that was *good*!"

"Come over here real quick. I wanna see if you can do the same thing but balancing me on your head."

Z started to snicker, but the pain behind her eyes forced her to stop. She rubbed her temples but couldn't stop watching Riverly zigzag toward the door.

Riverly ignored the jibes sent her way, which was basic survival for a pixie living among other pixies, and finally reached her destination. "We're not locked in. That's just what he *wants* us to think." She glanced over her shoulder and reached for the knob. "He can't *do* anything to us in here. He's just a—"

When her fingers touched the brass knob, the door flashed with the gnome's blue light. With a zap and a violent pop, Riverly was thrown away from the door. She hurtled across the room and smacked into the wall where the oversized mirror had been hung. With a squeak of flesh on glass and a hollow thud, the pixie crumpled to the floor in a heap.

Without being able to stop it.

Without using her magic.

What the hell?

Riverly groaned, which told them she was still breathing and would be okay. That assumed the magic that had blasted her across the room hadn't permanently affected her ability to heal. Also, her magic glow and her wings were gone.

Everyone's wings were gone.

Normally, that wouldn't have been a big deal. Hiding their wings was part of being a pixie when they wanted to fit in with the rest of human society. This was different.

The lack of ability to fly had caused Riverly to smack into the mirror on the wall like a bug hitting a windshield. Their wings were what made them pixies. They were integral and important.

Z glanced at Calinda to see if their leader looked as confused as she was.

She did. Then she glared at the door.

The others were slower on the uptake, but as they came to the same realization, the room filled with a cold, empty silence that felt bigger than the space.

"Riverly," Marv muttered, then slid his boot across the floor and gently nudged her thigh. "That was a joke, right?"

"If it was," Bird whispered, "it was the worst joke I've ever seen."

"A joke. Right, Riverly?"

The pixie gazed at Marv with welling eyes and shook her head.

"Aw, *hell*, no!" Bill struggled to his feet and stormed across the room to the door, managing a slightly straighter line than Riverly's. "Nobody takes our wings. You hear me out there? Nobody!"

When he reached the door, the three pixies closest to him leapt to their feet, shouted his name, and raced after him to prevent him from being magically electrocuted.

"It's not the door." Hasher peered over his shoulder into

the giant mirror. "I can't feel my wings. I can't even *see* 'em."

"Did you try letting your illusion down first?"

"What illusion? Before I woke up in here *without* wings, I was out in the woods *with* wings. Explain when I'd have time to cast an illusion spell. Tell me how that works."

"Damn, dude. Sorry I asked."

"I'm still big." Bird patted her face, shoulders, and abdomen as she gazed around the room. "I'm big! Why am I big?"

Kilder snapped his fingers multiple times, trying to cause a spark of magic to burst into life between them. It wouldn't come. "Aw, *shit*, man. Not even a little bit. It's gone."

That broke what was left of the pixies' composure, and the room erupted in shrieking outbursts. Anger and fear gripped all of them.

"*What?* Your magic's *gone?*"

"The gnome took our magic? How is that even *possible?*"

"I want it *back!*"

"No wings! No magic! No cute pixie-sized feet. Or hands. Or nose."

"Screw *cute*. When I get outta here, I'm gonna find that gnome. I'm gonna take his stick, and I'm gonna shove it up his—"

The disengaging of the door's lock made everyone go quiet. The knob turned, the door swung into the room, and in walked the old gnome, followed by a human in a military uniform whom none of the pixies had seen before. If he was one of the soldiers from the woods, he looked better than the others had when the pixies disappeared.

No, Z thought as she watched both newcomers enter the room. One was hunched over and gripped his walking stick for stability. The other was broad-shouldered and straight-faced as he surveyed the room. *This guy's not one of those soldiers. He looks way too full of himself to be a grunt.*

She couldn't figure out how the gang had gotten mixed up with the US military and what an officer like this one was doing running around with an old gnome and his psychotic walking stick.

CHAPTER SEVEN

The door, which was the pixies' only chance at escape, shut swiftly and decisively behind the mystery officer, and the room was silent.

The old gnome stood there, his beady eyes roaming from face to face among the clueless gang of pixies.

He's looking at us like we broke into this place and got caught red-handed. They don't have any evidence against us, and if we've been arrested, this is not legit.

Z studied the newcomers with a frown. The gnome looked cranky and irritable, like he'd given up his favorite pastime in the insanely early hours of a Thursday morning and would rather be anywhere else. The human looked like he had no idea what was going on but was doing his damnedest to act like he did.

"You're all here," the gnome muttered. "That's promising. Looks like everyone's awake, so we might as well get started."

"With what?" Calinda snapped, taking the lead for her

family of vagabond pixies and voicing what everyone had been wondering.

The wizened magical adjusted his grip on his walking stick and turned his head to meet their leader's gaze. "I offered the chance to have this chat on your turf. You refused." He shrugged. "Not that I expected a gang of ingrates like you to take me up on it, but now the game's changed. You're here until this gets done."

It was the wrong thing to say.

The pixies leapt to their feet, clenched their fists, and leaned forward aggressively, then attempted to wreak havoc on the strangers who'd knocked them out and kidnapped them. When it dawned on them that their magic was useless here, if not gone, they erupted in outrage.

"Who the hell do you think you are?"

"We don't owe you shit, Pops. Get lost!"

"This is harassment!"

"If you don't give us our magic back, we'll go straight to the—"

The old gnome slammed the butt of his walking stick down on the tile floor, and the resulting crack echoed. A burst of electric-blue light flared around the top, and the hunched magical's bushy eyebrows drew together. "Do we need to make your timeout longer, or are we good? I can do this all damn day, but I *really* don't want to."

No one said a word after that, which was impressive for a dozen pixies lacking their magic who were crammed into one room. The power the old gnome wielded was impressive too, both for getting the gang away from their home in the woods and being threatening enough to make them shut up.

The gnome nodded curtly. "Smart choice. Now, sit down."

Hasher was the only pixie who responded to the command. He was standing beside one of the metal chairs and pulled it out from under the table. The room filled with the grating squeal of metal, and he walked around the chair and plopped down on the seat.

The other pixies stopped glaring at the gnome to stare at him.

Hasher didn't seem to notice until Calinda whispered harshly, "Hasher. What are you doing? Stand up."

He started and leapt to his feet, then shuffled away from the chair and folded his arms as he cleared his throat.

Great, Z thought. *Now the guy with the superpowered stick thinks we're divided and that he's pinpointed our weakest link.*

When it came to starting trouble, Hasher was as skilled as his fellow gang members and any other pixie one might encounter. Getting out of trouble, on the other hand, was the green pixie's worst nightmare. During the time Z and her cousins had known him, he hadn't gotten it right.

The old gnome watched this byplay with amused detachment. He looked at Calinda and grunted in irritation or acceptance or maybe both. "Fine. Sit. Stand. I don't give a shit. As long as you face front and quit interruptin' every damn minute." He turned to offer the military officer a curt nod. "They're all yours, Major."

"Thank you."

It was weird that there was only one human in the

room. Him being there to lead them in a private chat, not the old gnome, was even weirder. Being a member of the military was the cherry on top of the kooky sundae.

Z frowned at the man, and he was unfortunate enough to get the look from the other eleven pixies trapped in the room with him. *What is this?* The crotchety old gnome wasn't giving anything away, so she and the others were forced to pay attention to the major.

He clasped his hands behind his back and cleared his throat. "My name is Major Winters," he began stiffly. "You're in the custody of the United States Army."

"Bullshit," Bill blurted.

The gnome with the stick only had to clear his throat to stop their onslaught of laughter and a slew of crude and insulting comments.

Winters didn't react as he searched the faces of the human-sized pixies standing angrily before him. He inhaled deeply and continued. "You've been busy little pixies lately. Before anybody asks, yes, I have proof, and yes, I know it's you. Here's how.

"Video footage in Albuquerque. Looked like just another bank robbery at first, but two of you started flying before you were out of the security camera's view.

"Eyewitness accounts of vandalism and looting in Oklahoma City, Kansas City, and St. Louis. Normally, that isn't a lot to go on, but when fifteen witnesses tell the same story without speaking to each other, it's hard to ignore.

"Then there was the art museum in Chicago, the aquarium in Boston, the Children's Museum in Portland—"

"Oh, *yeah*," Domino murmured as he glanced at the ceiling with a lazy smile. "That was a good night."

Bird let out a high-pitched giggle, then clapped both hands over her mouth and stared at the top of the gnome's walking stick. The elderly magical didn't seem as ready to send out another electric blast from his weapon, but nobody wanted to take a chance.

Still, some of the pixies chuckled at Domino's comment, and Z shot her cousin a sharp but amused look. *It's funny. He gets points for being clever, but if he doesn't stop while he's ahead, none of this is gonna be funny for much longer.*

Domino understood that, so he just smirked at her and spread his arms in a gesture that could have been an apology or in defense of his weakness for witty quips.

Z saw Echo give her brother the same kind of smirk. Then Major Winters started talking again.

"I know y'all are damn proud of yourselves for the trail of chaos and confusion y'all left in your wake. I could list another dozen instances of fraud, grand larceny, armed robbery, assault, burglary, and conspiracy to commit any combination of the above. Multiple instances. We've spent the last couple of months trying to get your gang tied down and locked up. Falling for a free robbery bag at the bank y'all trashed was as rookie a mistake as they come, but it's what led us to your hideout, so I'll take it."

At his mention of the tracking device, every pixie in the room turned to glare at Grulo. Aware of the silent shaming from the rest of his crew, the guilty pixie held up both middle fingers and waved them in opposite directions as he stared at nothing on the wall beside the door.

"Why are *you* here?" Z blurted, unable to sit on her

question any longer. The human was taking too long to get to the point.

Winters looked surprised by the out-of-turn question, but he recovered and cocked his head like he'd expected her to know the answer. "Well, to start, I'm in command of the team that found y'all out in the woods."

"Yeah, after weeks or months or however long of trying to find us." She folded her arms. "Not like I'm an expert, but I'm pretty sure the Army normally has nothing to do with bank robbers and everyday criminals. Or magicals. So, why are *you* talking to us instead of the FBI? They're the next step up from the local police, right?"

Kilder barked a laugh. "'Cause the local cops are dumb as hell. Duh."

The major looked stunned by the exchange, and his upper lip curled in disgust. "It's always the FBI first, isn't it?"

Interesting. Looks like I hit a sore spot with the guy who's giving us a serious talk. What happened between him and the FBI?

Winters managed to recover his air of commanding superiority, and he surprised Z and every other pixie by answering her question. Kind of.

"This is a special situation, and trust me. You're lucky to be in this room instead of shackled to a bench at the Bureau." The man stepped aside and gestured at the gnome, who was still leaning on his walking stick. "Carmine Ratchetter, our mutual friend—"

"Never seen him before in my life," Marv interjected.

When the major glared at him, Marv was quickly and

painfully elbowed in the ribs by Riverly. She gave him an even dirtier look to keep him from saying anything else.

Winters stared at him for another few seconds, then continued talking as if he hadn't been interrupted. "Has agreed to act as both consultant to the US Army and a mediator on behalf of certain Oriceran magicals here on Earth, specifically y'all."

"Mediator for what?" Calinda asked, sounding strong and confident despite their situation, even if she was neither.

Shit. She's worried. Z glanced across the room to find her cousins looking her way. It seemed they'd come to the same conclusion.

The room was silent as everyone waited for the answer.

The major looked like he was enjoying himself. He let the seconds draw out before answering. A humorless smile spread across his lips, which didn't improve the mood or the sense of impending doom that had the attention of the pixies.

"For what we're gonna do with a gang of rogue pixies who can't seem to figure out how things work on this planet." The man spread his arms, and his smile widened. "Human folks who take too many wrong turns get the local police. Multiple crimes crossing state lines with a long and irritating rap sheet like y'all's? Normally, the fellas at the Bureau would be all over it, but y'all ain't human, and the trouble y'all've caused over the last eight months isn't big or bothersome enough for the special agents with the Department of Magicals and Monsters to dirty their hands trying to clean up. Y'all with me so far?"

None of the pixies spoke, but Winters was the recipient

of a dozen hard, hateful stares. As a decorated major who had worked his way up through the ranks over the last forty years, a dozen stares laced with various flavors of "Drop dead, Major" were nothing new. When he thought about it, with the pixies' magic dampened in this room, negating their ability to act out, this felt more like addressing new recruits than a gang of magicals who'd neutralized one of his best Special Forces teams in seconds.

While they were two inches tall.

However, the ones with smart mouths kept those orifices shut…for now.

He nodded and continued his speech, feeling more confident by the second. "I'm just a human with a little sway when it comes to military decisions, but as it happens, I know a thing or two about *your* world and the way y'all operate. Oriceran had its own version of the FBI. The Silver Griffins, isn't that right? Hell, if y'all had started robbing banks and terrorizing towns a year ago, they would've scooped y'all up and handed out ultimatums.

"However, Carmine tells me the Silver Griffins aren't in business anymore. I don't pretend to understand Oriceran politics, so I won't ask for an explanation. Wouldn't change the facts anyway. Y'all are between a rock and a hard place right now.

"The Bureau isn't interested in small fry like pixies. Silver Griffins can't do a damn thing to help you *or* haul you away."

When the major turned to glance at Carmine, the old gnome raised an eyebrow and nodded curtly. That was the green light for the man to continue giving the rest of his long, drawn-out speech.

"Maybe y'all're thinking you just ran out of options." With a snort, Winters spread his arms again in what looked like a welcoming gesture. His tight, exaggerated grin sent a different message, though. "Lucky for y'all, the Army takes *all* kinds, which is why we're here in this room together, having so much fun."

CHAPTER EIGHT

What does he mean the Army takes all kinds?

Z turned to Calinda. The gang leader stood as still as everyone else, waiting for the major to drop the final bombshell. Her jaw was set and her eyes were narrowed at the blabbing human, but the color had drained from her cheeks. Z realized that whatever came next, none of them would like it.

Fortunately, Major Winters didn't make them wait any longer to hear what that was.

"Think of this as an experiment if you want. Y'all's *legal authority* is out of order for however long. Nobody else'll take you, and the brass wants to know what happens when the Army adds magicals to the Big Green Machine. Trying a different route to handle the bigger, more unbelievable national security threats the Bureau doesn't give a shit about since that *is* our job. What d'ya think?"

The gang of pixies tried to reconcile what they'd heard with what had been asked of them. Then Hasher scoffed, folded his arms, and turned to Grulo, who was standing beside him.

"Did you get any of that? I have no idea what he just said."

Grulo shrugged. "I mean, I knew humans had seriously weird beliefs, but he wants us to think he's following orders from *metal?*"

His reaction sparked another outburst of questions and comments from the pixies, none addressed to anyone in particular.

"What brass? Like, all of it in the world, or just a doorknob or…"

"Maybe it's telepathic brass?"

"That's not a thing here. Is it?"

"Gotta say, I'm not a fan of being thrown into *any* machine. Doesn't matter what color it is."

"Oh, shit. Are they gonna let us get small again and force us to keep a machine running? Like, from the *inside?* I saw this movie once where—"

Carmine smacked his walking stick on the floor again and cleared his throat. "Everybody shut up! This ain't a Q-and-A."

He didn't have to add the blue warning flash this time since the pixies had caught on to what happened following an outburst from the gnome. They quit talking so they wouldn't be magically electrocuted again or potentially teleported somewhere else, which was generally impossible for most magicals to accomplish.

"Major," Carmine grumbled, "get to the point."

"I was almost there." Winters glowered at the gnome's

bald head, but Carmine either didn't see it or didn't care. "Here's the deal, people. Pixies. Whatever. The Army's looking for magicals to join a special training and operations program. Y'all need somewhere to go that isn't prison and won't make your lives worse. Of course, you can go back to where you came from."

Bird clicked her tongue. "Back to Oriceran? Come on. You think we traveled between the worlds for fun?"

"With the way y'all've been destroying what's on this one? Yes." The major raised his eyebrows as he scanned every magical face turned toward him. "Y'all're free to go back to that planet of yours without any other consequences. It's a hell of a freebie. Or you can stay here on Earth, but it isn't free. If any of you wanna *stay*, you'll sign a contract and work for the United States Army."

"Great." Bill grimaced. "What's behind Door Number Three?"

Winters looked baffled by the question. "There is no—"

"You can stay in this room for the rest of your miserable lives," Carmine interrupted, stabbing a gnarled finger at the floor to emphasize his point. "No magic. No shrinking. No flying."

Marv raised an eyebrow and scrutinized the old gnome. "You know what I think? I think you're full of shit."

Carmine continued his description of their third option as if no one had said a word. As he spoke, it became clear it wasn't really an option.

"Three square meals a day, *if* the boys making the grub here remember you exist. You *might* have a bed. Depends on whether there's enough to go around on any given day.

No toilet in here, so it'll probably end up bein' a bucket. Two, if you're lucky.

"That's it. No fresh air, no sunshine, no mischief. You can keep *not* making decisions as long as you damn well please since that's the only thing you're gettin' if you don't choose one of the major's two options. *Capisce?*"

Marv's eyes had widened while the old gnome had given his explanation of "Door Number Three." None of it sounded appealing, but the worst part was the idea of being locked into one room for the rest of their magical life. Pixies lived a very long time.

Marv swallowed, his face a mask of terror. "Yeah, okay."

With an exasperated grunt, Carmine shook his head, then bumped the end of his walking stick against the major's arm. "'Bout time to wrap this thing up."

"Right." Winters nodded and surveyed his potential recruits one more time. "Y'all got a decision to make, and you'll stay in the Army's custody until it's made. Throw your hat in with me and mine, or take that one-way ticket back to Oriceran. I'll give y'all some time to think it over."

With a curt nod, the major turned his back on the gang and left the room. Carmine, however, stayed behind.

Z assumed that in his role as mediator, the old gnome felt obliged to stick around in case the pixies had questions that only another magical could answer. However, he didn't give them a chance to ask questions, and he didn't offer unsolicited advice.

The only vibe Z got from the old magical was that he didn't want to be here. When he finally opened his mouth to impart a few final words, the pixies hung on them.

"He's not screwin' around, you know. You little shits've caused big problems, and you're gonna have to make up for it one way or the other. Personally, I like this planet. If you wanna stay, the major's deal is a decent chance to turn your shit around. Be better.

"You know as well as I do what we all left behind on Oriceran. The details don't matter. If you give a damn about where you end up, don't treat this like a joke."

Calinda sighed. "They're just humans. Not even dangerous ones. We kicked their asses in the woods. They can't force us to choose."

Lifting his chin to peer at her, Carmine shuffled slowly across the room, his stick clacking with every other step along the way. The other pixies cleared a path for him so he could get to their leader. She peered down at the old gnome with a deep frown, her lips firmly pressed together.

When he reached the fuchsia-haired pixie, Carmine murmured, "If it were just the humans, dangerous or not, you would be right. But in case you haven't noticed, they have help, and their consultant *is* qualified to make sure every one of you decides on *something*."

Most magicals being stared down by Carmine Ratchetter would have found their resolve quickly crumbling, but Calinda didn't blink. Pixies were as well-known for fearlessness as for creating mischief and chaos. She did lower her voice, either to make herself sound more intimidating or to keep the others from hearing the conversation. Unfortunately, the room was small enough that it was impossible not to hear every word.

"If you really came from Oriceran," she began, her voice

tinged with a warning, "you know we can't go back. There's nothing left for us there."

"I do know that." The old gnome studied her face. "I might be the only magical ever to say this to a pixie, but I trust you and yours'll make the right choice."

He started to leave, but he paused when his gaze fell on the gaudy necklace around her throat, winking in the fluorescent lights. Moving faster than a magical of his age and physical infirmity should have been able to, he pointed at the necklace, then light flared around it. The clasp undid itself, and the piece of jewelry fell into his clawed hand.

He shot Calinda a final uncompromising look and grumbled, "Starting with giving *this* back to whoever it belongs to."

She didn't try to stop him as he hobbled away, his walking stick rhythmically striking the tile floor.

Before he reached the door, Calinda called after him, "We're pixies, gnome. We don't work for anyone but ourselves, and we don't take orders. You know that, and deep down in that grizzled old body of yours, you have a conscience."

Carmine had turned the knob and opened the door wide enough for a gnome with a walking stick to pass through. He paused for what felt like a long time, and Calinda took it as an opportunity to drive her point home.

"When we tell that human to stick it where the sun don't shine, I know you'll do the right thing. You won't force us to go back to Oriceran."

He didn't turn to face her. "Wanna bet?" The old gnome didn't spare any of them a glance after delivering that line, which was nothing short of a promise. The door closed on its own as the Army's magical consultant shuffled down the hall.

Silence filled the room like toxic gas, building until they couldn't take it anymore. Bill drew a long, hissing breath through his teeth.

"We're fucked."

CHAPTER NINE

Major Winters had told the pixies they'd have time to think about the Army's offer before making their decision, but he'd failed to mention how long.

In true pixie fashion, most of Calinda's gang didn't take their predicament seriously. They continued pretending they didn't believe that the old gnome Carmine would hold to the major's word and send them back to Oriceran if they didn't agree to join the Army.

The thought was absurd, even for pixies, and that was saying something.

"Human doesn't know what he's talking about," Marv murmured as he shook his head. "Thinks taking on a bunch of pixies is gonna give him his own version of the FBI's…what did he call it? Department of Monsters?"

"What do *you* know about it?"

"I've heard things, all right? Couple elves from Cali or whatever, and this dwarf who made a big splash a couple years ago. Jack Daniels or Jose Cuervo or something like that."

"Dude, *what*?"

"I don't know. He's got the same name as some kinda booze! You think I care enough to remember it?"

"Doesn't matter what his name is," Calinda cut in wryly. "This is a different situation."

"How? The FBI's been hiring magicals to do their shitwork for a couple decades now. How's this any different?"

"You mean other than that it's the Army versus the FBI?"

"Shut up, Riverly. I wasn't asking you."

"It's *different* because the FBI isn't bringing in magicals and turning them into brand-new federal agents with a high security clearance and access to the Bureau's resources. They have the Bounty Hunter Division. There's a separation there. Contracted labor."

"Oy, gimme a break!"

"Winters is saying that if we wanna stay on Earth, we gotta hand over our lives to the Army and whatever dumb machine he was talking about. As in, they'll own us."

"How do you know *that*?"

"Have you ever *heard* a soldier talk about being in the Army?"

"No. But…ha. Judging by the way those soldiers were groaning in the woods, it's hard to believe they *like* their job."

That got a healthy dose of chuckles from the closest pixies. Then the conversation continued like it usually did when important decisions were left to the whole gang to make. Calinda was their leader, but she was as far from a dictator as the head of a rogue pixie gang could get.

Normally, every magical in their merry and mischievous band was included in the decision-making process. Today, however, three of Calinda's pixies didn't join the other nine in their huddle around the steel table.

Z and her cousins formed their own huddle. For the first time since Calinda's gang had agreed to take in the trio of transients they called "the triplets," what was best for Z and her cousins might not be what was best for the rest of the group.

She'd known that when Major Winters mentioned a forced return to Oriceran as an option for anyone who didn't take his deal. That realization was apparent on Domino's and Echo's faces when they joined her in the far corner of the room for as much of a private chat as the small space allowed.

Z didn't know how to kick off a conversation that was going to change their lives and how they'd chosen to spend their existence on this planet over the last hundred years. At first, it seemed easier to stand in a tight, three-pixie circle in the corner with their heads bowed toward each other while they listened to the heated arguments going on among the others.

Those kept Z and her cousins from having to say anything or finalizing their decision. However, she knew the decision had been made and the results of their three-pixie vote would be unanimous.

Before Z got the courage to say what they were all thinking out loud and in plain English, Domino saved her the effort by beating her to it.

"We can't go back to Oriceran," he murmured.

"I know," she replied, nodding.

"I don't care what Calinda says or if everyone else hates

us for it. They might call us traitors. They might even disown us, and then we're on our own."

"I know. Trust me. I've been over it in *my* head too." Z nodded, glancing between Domino's concerned expression and Echo's blank face.

The goth pixie generally looked like she didn't give a shit about anything, but those who knew her understood that intense, focused eye contact without blinking was Echo's tell when something had gotten her attention. Nothing got Echo's attention unless she cared about it.

"I already know my answer," he continued, "But the question has to be asked. If we do this…" Domino glanced over his cousin's shoulder at the rest of the gang, who were still huddled around the table. "I just wanna make sure we all get it. We'll be losing a second family, you know? You guys think you can handle that?"

Echo clicked her tongue and grimaced in disgust.

"Hey, I'm not trying to be condescending. Honest. But, like, if we do this without laying out all the facts, one of you's gonna get pissed as hell when it doesn't turn out the way you…*ow!*" He tried to jerk away from his sister's elbow-jab in the ribs, but standing in the corner of the room prevented him from getting as far from her as he would have liked. "Hey!"

Echo glared at him. She didn't need to whisper in his ear to get her point across.

Domino rubbed his sore ribs and chuckled. "Aw, come on. I'm not saying you're idiots and can't think of the pros and cons on your own. I'm just saying…you know." He shrugged and looked at Z. "Sometimes we dive into things without knowing what to expect, and it doesn't turn out that great. That's all."

"Well, I think this is different than trying to decide what's for dinner or which part of the gang's next house we're gonna claim." Z raised an eyebrow, and Echo snorted without changing her expression. "You laid out the cons of staying on Earth, but one serious pro outweighs all of them."

Nodding, Echo pointed at Z and gave her brother a poignant look.

Domino's eyebrows drew together, making him look even more concerned. "You guys are fine with leaving everyone else behind just like that? Losing another family? Maybe never being able to talk to them again? If this Army crap doesn't work out, we're cut off from everybody else we know."

Z looked over her shoulder at the rest of the crew. None of them seemed worried about the triplets having their own huddle in the corner. Z and her cousins did that, and the rest of the pixies had gotten used to it. It also meant that nobody suspected a thing.

It's gonna be hard to let them down like this, but they'll understand. If they don't, it won't matter anyway. They'll be back on Oriceran, and I'll be keeping my promise.

When she faced her cousins again, the siblings' identical expressions of concern and anticipation would have been comical under different circumstances.

After taking a deep breath, she nodded. "Okay, first, do I *want* to say goodbye to another family? Of course not. We were lucky to find these guys when we got to this planet, and I love 'em as much as you do. You're right, though,

Dom. We *can't* go back to Oriceran, even if it means taking Winters' crazy deal."

After a moment of silent consideration, Echo whispered her thoughts and concerns in her brother's ear. He looked surprised, then met her gaze.

"Are we sure there aren't any other options? Yeah, Echo. I mean, can you come up with a genius new plan to get us out of this before the human comes back to make us choose? The gnome made it pretty damn clear what the only other option was, and it's the worst one."

"We're staying here," Z added in a tone of finality.

The cousins' return gazes made it clear how closely related they were.

I have to remind them why we're doing what we have to do. Why I'm the one calling the shots here.

"Look, I made you guys a promise that night after…" Grimacing, she stopped and tried again. "Well, you remember."

Her cousins knew what she was talking about. Losing their entire family, all their blood relatives, in one violent night was something you didn't forget even when it had been over a hundred years since then.

They didn't say anything, but they were listening. Z had to finish what she'd been trying to say. "Before we left Oriceran, I promised you that I'd always look out for you. That we'd stick together no matter what, and we'd do whatever we had to do to keep each other safe from then on. We promised *each other* that we were never going back to Oriceran, so that's not even an option. Calinda's been really good to us since we got here. So has everyone else, but keeping *us* together is more important than not breaking up the gang."

The confidence and assuredness she spoke with surprised her, but it was better to sound confident than clueless.

Z shrugged and added, "But I don't own you, so if you have a different opinion, now is the time to share."

Domino and Echo exchanged quick, silent glances, which was all they needed to do to be on the same page. "We're with you on this, Z. All in."

His sister nodded for emphasis, still looking neither excited nor anywhere near as regretful as she had now they'd decided what their next move was going to be.

"Okay. Good." Z attempted to smile, but it didn't feel convincing. She broke their huddle to lean against the wall beside the giant mirror.

"So..." Domino shoved his hands into the front pockets of his dark-green corduroys and raised his eyebrows. "How do you wanna tell everybody?"

Z looked at the pixies around the table, all of whom seemed to be in high spirits. That was probably because they'd come to their own decision. *They're taking it for granted that my cousins and I will roll with whatever they decide like we always have.*

"We don't," she muttered flatly.

"What?" He dropped his voice and leaned toward her. "I think they deserve to know, Z. Don't you?"

"Of course they do, and they'll find out when we tell Winters we're staying. If they know before that, they're gonna do everything they can to convince us we're making the wrong choice."

CHAPTER TEN

They couldn't tell how long they'd been locked inside the room before Winters returned to hear their decision.

To Z, it felt like they'd been in there for a full day, maybe longer. She wasn't looking forward to the looks on the others' faces when she told the major in front of everyone that she and her cousins would *not* be taking that one-way trip back to Oriceran.

Waiting was always the hardest part, and it was worse for pixies.

When the room's door opened again, everyone stood and faced the entrance, expecting the grumpy old gnome to come in first. However, the human walked in alone and shut the door behind him. Carmine was nowhere to be seen.

"Figured y'all been in here long enough to reach a decision," he stated matter-of-factly as he folded his arms. "If not, I can come back in another couple of hours. I have time."

"No, we're ready." Calinda stepped between the gang

and the human who was offering them two bad options now they'd been caught for their crimes. It took an extraordinary effort for her to face him with a modicum of respect, even though no pixie appreciated being forced into a corner. "I have one question for you first."

"All right."

She smiled bitterly. "Did you think you could round up a bunch of pixies, toss around threats, and get them to pick your side?"

Winters blinked and took a sharp breath. "Honestly, I didn't have any idea that this would go one way or the other, but I *was* warned against getting my hopes up."

"That's good advice. Hope you followed it. You got a gang of pixies to ship off to another planet."

The major peered at her, his expression blank. "How many?"

"Twelve." Calinda spread her arms and shrugged. "Unless you're planning on picking up more magical miscreants along the way."

"Fair enough. Looks like y'all made your choice—"

"Actually, Major," Z interrupted. She stepped out of the far corner of the room. "Whatever it takes to send someone back through the gates, you're only gonna need it for nine pixies."

The man turned toward her like he thought he was imagining the whole thing. Calinda didn't move, just shot Z a sidelong glance. A murmur of surprise and confusion spread through the rest of the gang.

"I get three outta the bunch, huh?" Winters eyed Z. "I assume one of those three is you."

"And my cousins," she replied, jerking a thumb to either

side to indicate Domino on her right and Echo on her left. "We're not going back to Oriceran, so I guess that means we're taking your deal."

"I guess it does." He gave her cousins the same blank, unimpressed look, then nodded. "Y'all have any military experience?"

Z scowled at him. "You didn't say that was a requirement."

"No, I didn't. Doesn't stop me from being curious enough to ask, though."

What does he care about military experience? That wasn't part of the deal, and threats from a human aren't gonna get me or my cousins to talk about what we lost and how.

So, instead of divulging the full truth to a human stranger in front of the other nine pixies, Z went with a much smaller sliver.

"We had something to do with taking out that team of Special Ops soldiers in the woods, in case you forgot."

One of the other pixies barked a laugh and tried to cover it. Several others snickered.

Domino dipped his head to hide his smile.

Echo remained impassive.

Z held the major's gaze and shrugged. "I'm assuming that counts for something."

He didn't immediately do or say anything, and it started to feel like she'd entered a staring contest without being told about it. Then he clicked his tongue, sighed, and turned to the door again. "Noted. Y'all enjoy your night in holding."

"Wait a minute, *what?*" Bill interjected. "You're holding us here even longer?"

"You can't do that, man. Come on."

"We said we're going peacefully."

"Hey, human. You can keep the triplets. They actually *wanna* stay. Let the rest of us bounce, huh?"

The door opened under Winters' hand, and he turned halfway around for a final once-over of the shouting pixies. He didn't explain himself, not even to the three who'd elected to stay on Earth to become the US Army's first magical soldiers. When the door shut behind him with a soft click and the metallic clunk of the lock engaging, the gang was left to their own devices again for who knew how long.

Amidst the irritation and resentment and angry shouts in the room, Z glanced at Calinda. The gang leader was staring at her. When she raised her fuchsia eyebrows, it was clear that she was asking, "Are you sure?"

If she asked me why, I wouldn't be able to tell her. Not the whole truth. Yeah, I'm sure.

Z nodded once, and Calinda echoed the gesture, then rejoined the portion of her crew who would head back to their home planet when Major Winters released them. Nine would travel instead of the full dozen Calinda's band of rogue pixies had numbered for over a century.

She hadn't realized how nervous she'd been about what would happen when she relayed their decision, but now that Calinda knew they were splitting up and her reaction had been benign, Z felt a weight lift from her shoulders. Without the ability to blame magic or the thrill of flight, the only thing that could have lifted that weight was relief.

After shutting the door of a holding room filled with its strangest and most outrageous occupants to date, Major Winters walked swiftly down the hall. He checked his watch, then stopped at the next door on his left and opened it with a jerk.

Since it was part of their plan, he knew the old gnome was waiting for him. That didn't make the sight of Carmine Ratchetter in an Army facility less weird.

The old gnome was not your usual Army consultant. Hunched over and requiring his walking stick to move, he could call powerful magic at the drop of a hat.

Don't think I'll ever get used to it, the major thought. *Not with this guy.*

Winters pulled the door gently shut, then crossed the room and stopped at the gnome's side.

For a full minute, they stared through the two-way mirror built into the wall. From this side, the large rectangle was a tinted window through which a dozen rogue pixies were visible.

Carmine had switched off the audio, but Winters didn't need to hear what was being said in perceived solitude to know that none of the magical criminals were happy about their current circumstances.

Even the three who were taking the major up on his unexpected offer.

He studied them through the tinted glass. If he hadn't been told what they were, not to mention having seen the individuals in that room use magic against one of his elite teams, Winters would have assumed he was looking at yet another trio of miscreants.

The three were an odd collection: one goth chick, one

average-looking guy in corduroys and a long-sleeved plaid button-down shirt who looked like he belonged on a college campus, and a woman with vivid blue hair. They all looked like they were in their early- to mid-twenties.

Winters knew better than to trust the apparent age of a non-human. Magicals lived much longer than the norm. He'd given up trying to guess ages a long time ago.

Hearing one hundred, four hundred, or seven hundred years tossed around with the same condescension as, "Give him a break, he's only sixteen," made the fifty-eight-year-old human feel more insignificant than usual, even after more than two-thirds of his life in the Army.

He wouldn't ask their ages since they didn't matter when it came down to implementing his plans for the Oriceran Integration Program. He just needed pixies brave or desperate enough to accept the offer. He would learn their names soon.

Especially the girl with blue hair. That one looks like a magical fury bomb waiting to go off. Can't be all that different to handle than the kind without magic, and I've seen plenty of those roll through my ranks.

That didn't mean the initial phase of his program was going to be easy. Starting with three would likely make it a lot more difficult, but three was all he had. He couldn't turn them away just because the number who'd accepted his deal didn't match his hypothetical ideal.

Silently standing beside an old gnome, spying on a dozen pixies in Army custody, eventually got to be too much for him. Winters cleared his throat, then lifted a hand to stroke his beardless chin since it made him feel contemplative. Hopefully, it made him look less uncertain about this as well.

"It's a lot less than I expected, honestly," he muttered, forcing himself to keep staring blankly through the window despite how badly he wanted to look at the gnome. He knew Carmine Ratchetter didn't give away his thoughts, and searching the gnome's face for what he knew he'd never find would make the major look desperate. "You think three's enough?"

Carmine snorted. "If you ask me, that's three too many, but you made your bed with 'em, Major. Now you gotta lie in it."

A pang of regret bordering on panic shot through the major, countering the medications he was taking for high blood pressure. *Buyer's remorse isn't allowed, old son. This is called making history. Pull yourself together.*

He couldn't help asking, "Why? There something wrong with those three I should know about before we start?"

The gnome blinked, then braced his walking stick on the tile floor to support himself while he turned to face him. Carmine stared at Winters in disbelief, like he was waiting for the human's stoic expression to break so they could laugh at the joke.

"Something *wrong* with 'em?" Carmine chuckled. "They're *pixies*, Major. Not a whole hell of a lot that *ain't* wrong with 'em. Just you wait."

With a curt nod, the gnome shuffled past Winters, satisfied with this end to their conversation. Winters didn't agree. He turned to watch the wizened magical cross the room. "Where are you going?"

"I'm hungry. Last time I checked, a military consultant didn't need permission to leave a room or stuff his face in the mess hall. Or did the rules change?"

Winters shook his head and returned to watching the pixies. "Have a nice dinner, then."

"Probably not." The door creaked open, and Carmine gave a laugh that sounded more ominous than amused. "Might as well wish you luck right now, Major. You're gonna need it more than they will."

"Uh-huh." The major didn't turn away from the window. "We'll see about that."

That made the old gnome pause, then he threw his head back and howled. His laughter didn't stop as he hobbled out of the room, and he didn't bother to close the door behind him.

That made it easy for Major Winters to hear the old magical muttering to himself as he shuffled down the hall. "We'll see. We'll *see?* Ha! His own stupidity! Like he could pull this off with three pixies and actually have it go his way. *We'll see!*"

When the gnome's words faded, Winters was left with the distinct impression the Army's magical consultant was trying to make him feel horrible on purpose. "What else is new?"

CHAPTER ELEVEN

Z hadn't expected Major Winters to leave her and her cousins in the room with the rest of Calinda's crew after they'd accepted his offer, but when her soon-to-be new boss exited, she realized that she, Domino, and Echo weren't going to be carted off and immediately inducted.

She was concerned about what might happen.

Calinda and the rest of the crew had always been accepting and kind, or as accepting and kind as pixies could be. They'd been family. They'd also developed a reputation for overreacting and going the extra mile to even the score if they felt they'd been slighted, mistreated, or disrespected. That reputation had been well-established when Z and her cousins came into the picture.

While they'd been family for over a hundred years, she expected it to be as easy for the other nine pixies to turn on her and her cousins for agreeing to Major Winters' terms as it had been for the triplets to separate themselves from the crew.

For the first time in a long time, what Z expected and what happened were two different things.

The rest of the pixies acted like nothing had changed. Like their three newest members hadn't decided to go against the grain and whittle the gang back to its original nine. Not only that, but they brought the triplets into all their jokes, stories told to pass the time, and crude insults aimed at Carmine Ratchetter and Major Winters and the US Army.

Not one of them looked angry or resentful after hearing Z and her cousins' decision, although she wondered if the lack of useable magic in this room accounted for everyone being in an accepting mood.

When the door opened long enough to deliver an open cardboard box filled with single-serving dinners in Ziplock bags, the triplets were given their meals as quickly as everyone else. No one tried to get a jab in or make Z feel worse about a decision that had been hard to make.

No one talked about what would happen after they were released, though. It was clear that they'd go their separate ways. Calinda and the original nine were heading back to Oriceran to wreak havoc on their home planet, and Z and her cousins would remain on Earth and start a new life in the military, whatever that entailed.

All things considered, it couldn't have turned out better since none of them could go back in time and not get caught.

At this point, the only real complaints were that their meals sucked and the holding room was starting to stink.

They'd been through worse, however.

Knowing the rest of the group didn't harbor any ill will

made it easier to fall asleep despite the lack of beds, pillows, or blankets. Z had been prepared to stay up all night. It wouldn't have been the first time circumstances had forced her to take protective measures for herself and her cousins.

By the time the fluorescent lights in the room shut off and the conversations died, she knew that wouldn't be necessary. Calinda's rogue dozen would spend their last night together as a crew, and tomorrow, they'd go their separate ways. Probably forever.

The next morning, none of the pixies was surprised to find Major Winters was making them wait even longer for their inevitable release just because he could. A soldier slid another cardboard box of Ziplocked breakfasts into the room.

After that, they waited for an indeterminate length of time—between two and seven hours was the consensus—before they were approached by another living being.

When Major Winters opened the door, he didn't walk into the room to join them. He stood out in the hall and barked at them through the doorway,

"Final call for anyone shipping off-planet. If you haven't said your goodbyes, you have five minutes to wrap them up. Then you'll head out with Sergeant Manney and Sergeant Paulson here. Clock's ticking."

The pixies shot each other amused looks, chuckling at the major's odd address as the man stepped out of the doorway. He was replaced by two soldiers, the aforementioned sergeants, who stood side by side, hands clasped behind their backs.

When the pixies didn't move, they stood where they

were, watching and listening to everything that happened inside the holding room for the next five minutes.

Only then did Calinda and her gang remind her people that they wouldn't all be heading down that hall. The leader kicked off the goodbyes by heading to the back corner, where Z and her cousins were waiting for whatever came next.

"Craziest century I've had in a long time." Calinda thrust her hand toward Z. "I think the three of you had something to do with it."

Z couldn't help laughing as she clasped the other's hand. "Or maybe we were just along for the ride."

"Yeah. Maybe." Calinda shook Domino's hand next, then Echo's. "You take care of yourselves down here. And if you ever *do* come home, you know how to find us."

"Thanks, Calinda."

Echo whispered in her brother's ear, and he relayed, "She says we'll miss all of you."

The gang leader chuckled as she turned away to head for the door. "Of course you will."

Marv approached them next and raised a hand to high-five each in turn. "Later, triplets." Echo didn't smack her hand against his but punched him in the shoulder. He let out a yip of surprise and pain and rubbed his shoulder.

Domino nodded at him. "She says two for flinching."

"What? No. She didn't tell *you*...*ow*! Hey!"

Echo sent two more quick jabs into Marv's shoulder and grinned. Her brother shrugged. "She was thinking it."

"Pshh. Right. Those soldiers are gonna *love* you."

"Give 'em hell, Z," Bird offered when it was her turn to grab Z's hand and say a quick goodbye.

The blue-haired pixie couldn't manage to smile, but she nodded. "That's the plan."

"Shouldn't be too hard," Domino added.

One by one, the rest of their chosen family came to the far corner of the room to say farewell. They'd gone over the five-minute time limit before half the pixies had said goodbye and stepped into the hallway, but neither of the sergeants waiting for them said anything about it or tried to hurry the process.

If they're doing that on purpose, they get that we probably won't see these pixies again. Ever. What's a few extra minutes when you're about to ship a bunch of magicals back to the planet they came from? Z thought.

Bill brought up the end of the line. He paused in front of Z and her cousins, then stuck out his hand and gave her a crooked smile. "Guess this is it, then."

"Guess it is." Z grabbed his hand for a firm shake, which Bill took a step further by squeezing around her fingers much harder than a handshake required.

"Gonna miss you," he muttered, holding her gaze.

She grinned and returned the squeeze with ten times the pressure. "You too, Bill."

He tried his hardest to keep a straight face, but then he reached his pain-and-pressure threshold and grimaced. "Okay, okay. We're good. I'm done."

As her cousins snickered behind her, Z released Bill's hand and let him tend to the crushing ache in his hand.

"Damn." With an uncertain chuckle, he shook out his reddened fingers and looked her up and down. "Won't miss *that*, though."

"Yeah, right," Domino remarked. "Take care of yourself, Bill."

"Well, *now*..." The pixie turned away from the triplets, cradling his hand and pretending to be in a lot more pain than he was.

Z watched the last of the gang walk out of their holding room and be ushered away by the two Army sergeants. They were going to Oriceran via the closest entryway through the interplanetary gates.

Her smile faded when one of the sergeants took one step inside the room to grab the doorknob and haul the door shut again. "Hey. What about us?"

The sergeant paused with the door half-closed. "What *about* you? You're staying."

"Yeah, but..." She glanced around the room. "Not in here."

"Well, nobody told me to let you out, so yeah." He looked around the room too, then sarcastically raised his eyebrows, "In here." He pulled the door shut.

Z stared at the closed door, then snorted. "Seriously?"

Biting her lower lip, Echo stared at the door. Since it was just the three of them, she could speak out loud. "Something tells me we'll get a lot of that in the near future."

With a sigh, Z folded her arms. "Yeah, no kidding."

"Aw, come on, guys." Domino looked at his sister and his cousin and shrugged, his crooked smile growing. "It's a human army. Can't be *that* bad, right?"

CHAPTER TWELVE

If this was their first taste of what their life would be like in the Army, it was going to be as bad as Echo predicted.

Z and her cousins were left to wait in the holding room for another twelve hours at a guess, assuming the soldiers who showed up to slide three plastic trays of food through the open door—once for lunch and again for dinner—were working on a "six hours between meals" schedule.

"This better not be all there is," Z muttered as she spooned up a glob of what she thought was mashed potatoes and gravy. She couldn't bring herself to put the spoon in her mouth.

"I don't know what you're talking about," Domino muttered, then shoveled in several forkfuls of the second and third types of mash on his plate. "This stuff is delicious."

Echo looked up from her tray, which she'd placed in front of her crossed legs. The edges of the tray lined up with the lines of grout on the tile floor. "I can't eat this."

"Why?" Her brother crammed two more bites into his mouth. "It's not *poison* or anything."

When the words left his lips, Domino paused with his fork halfway to his mouth. He sat up straight, stared at the mess of food covering the plastic tray, which had separators to keep things from touching each other, and swallowed his current mouthful.

"Right?" He looked at Z, who was sitting at the opposite end of the table.

She shrugged. "No magic in here, Dom."

Echo tilted her head with a sympathetic smile. "No way to tell if they're trying to poison us unless you drop dead in the next few hours. Then we'd know."

"Dammit." Domino dropped his fork on the tray and slumped in the chair. "I'm your *brother*. Why would you say something like that?"

Echo looked confused. "Being my brother doesn't make you immune to poison."

Z snorted, and when Domino shot her a scathing look, she shrugged. "Maybe it does. As far as we know, you've never *been* poisoned, so I guess we'll find out."

"You guys think you're so funny." Shaking his head, Domino dropped his gaze to the largely empty tray in front of him and added, "You're not."

He only lasted another five seconds before his appetite got the better of him. He leaned forward and shoveled the rest of his dinner into his mouth.

Z and Echo didn't touch theirs, but neither was hungry after breakfast *and* lunch *and* dinner the night before. It was more food in a twenty-four-hour period than they'd eaten in weeks.

"Anyone else feel like we traded being locked up as part of a pixie gang for being locked up as military prisoners?" Z asked as she watched Domino finish the last of his dinner. "Even *with* the food."

"They probably forgot about us," Echo replied in her flat, emotionless voice. "Can't tell if that's a good thing or a bad thing yet."

"Guess we'll have to keep waiting for that, too."

"They didn't forget about us," Domino interjected as he dropped his fork on the tray to signify that he'd eaten every last scrap. Then he leaned back in his chair and gestured at the empty tray. "Or they wouldn't have brought us two meals since everyone else left."

"Since they took everyone else *away*," Z interjected. "There's a difference."

"Maybe not," Echo added, staring blankly at the floor tiles in front of her. "Maybe the humans only told us what we wanted to hear. Maybe 'a one-way ticket back to Oriceran' was an esoteric euphemism."

Domino raised an eyebrow. "A what?"

The goth pixie looked at her brother, still expressionless. "Maybe they're *not* sending Calinda and everyone else through the gates, and when they were talking about one-way tickets, they meant energetically, not physically."

"Z." Domino met his cousin's gaze across the table and pointed at his sister. "You have any idea what this is?"

Z shrugged and shook her head.

Echo kept murmuring in her airy, spaced-out voice. "They'd have to be operating under the assumption that all Oricerans have a soul and that all souls return to their planet of origin. It'd be a lot faster and easier than escorting nine pixies to an opening through the gates." She paused, then flicked her gaze at her brother. "Ever heard of a firing squad?"

Domino and Z stared at the goth in silence, then he snorted and shook his head. "Fuck, you're morbid."

Z smiled and dropped her gaze to the steel tabletop.

Echo shrugged. "Sounds like a practical solution to me."

"Really? Catch a bunch of pixies and make 'em an offer, then kill 'em just 'cause it's *practical*. That's what you're going with?"

"Fewer meals to cook, and they didn't have to haul around a cardboard box of baggies today. Just trays for the three of us."

Domino shook his head. "We agreed to stay, and Winters agreed to send everyone else back to Oriceran."

"Did anyone get that in writing?" Despite the off-putting topic of conversation, his sister looked unfazed by the idea. "'Cause nobody stated *where* the others would be taken or what's gonna happen to us."

"She has a point," Z cut in, trying not to laugh.

Domino looked at them, then slapped both hands on the table and shoved his chair back before standing. "Okay, you're both screwing with me."

Z chuckled, and he paced across the room. Echo shrugged and went back to staring at her untouched dinner tray.

Fortunately, Domino had little time to ruminate on the possibilities his sister had brought to his attention. The door opened with a soft click, and Major Winters walked in. He had a thick manila folder tucked under his arm. The old gnome had joined him this time.

We're getting special treatment from the magical go-between? Z tried to keep a straight face as the major and the gnome headed toward the table, looking business-like. *What do they think we're gonna do?*

"Thanks for waiting," Winters said when he reached the table and dropped the stuffed folder on the surface.

"Yeah," Z replied wryly. "Good thing you decided to show. We were getting ready to pack up, call it a day, and head home."

Domino snorted. Echo looked up from her seat on the floor and studied the major's reaction.

Carmine was pulling out a chair but paused at Z's sarcastic response.

Major Winters met her gaze and sucked in a sharp breath of realization. "Oh. You just made a joke. That was it?"

She just held the man's gaze. *He's starting to get it.*

With a grunt, Carmine pulled his chair out the rest of the way and lowered himself onto the hard seat. "Starting off on the right foot. Good for you."

Winters ignored him in favor of opening the front of the manila folder and scanning the first piece of paper within it. After several seconds, his gaze still on the paperwork, he said flatly, "Everybody take a seat."

Z was sitting across from the major, but neither of her cousins moved. Winters didn't say it again, and he didn't look up from the folder.

Carmine spun his walking stick in one hand and raised his eyebrows in a silent but effective warning.

Okay, fine. We took the deal. I guess it's time to start acting like it.

Z looked at Domino, and her cousin grudgingly headed for the table. When she shot the same silent gaze at Echo, the goth didn't move.

Come on, she thought. *This is what we said we were gonna do.*

The old gnome picked up Echo's hesitation and thumped his walking stick on the floor, then cleared his throat. He didn't have to look at the young pixie to make his point clear. She could get up and join everyone else at the table, or he and his superpowered stick would *make* her.

Every pixie Carmine had captured and transported from the woods knew the old gnome was capable of delivering on his threat. That knowledge was the only thing that got Echo onto her feet and heading toward the table.

A tiny smirk graced the major's lips until the drawn-out ear-splitting screech of a metal chair being inched across the floor tiles wiped it off his face. Echo stared at him the whole time, being as loud and obnoxious as possible while doing what he asked.

Z forced herself to stare straight ahead while the terrible sound echoed through the room. *I wish I'd thought of that.*

When the noise stopped, Echo plopped down on the chair to Z's right and sat straight and still.

Major Winters' gaze slid left and right as he marked the pixies' faces. He shot Carmine a glance, but the gnome was involved in a staring contest with the people who were about to become the Army's first magical soldiers.

The major pulled multiple sheets of paper out of the file and divided them into three stacks, which he laid out in a line in front of him. "First things first. Once the paperwork's out of the way, I will put you to work."

He slid a stack of papers to each of the pixies. "Those are for you to sign. I assume all three of you know how to read."

Z looked at him sharply. "And I assumed a team of elite soldiers in the forest would be harder to put down. I guess we're all figuring things out the hard way."

Domino snorted as he looked at his cousin and the surprised-looking major. Echo started reading their unique contract with the Army as if she hadn't heard the exchange.

Carmine sat back in his chair and gazed appraisingly at the pixie who had been dumb *and* brave enough to talk smack to the military officer who'd apprehended her.

Winters took it in stride. This wasn't the first time he'd sat down with a soldier who had a hard time letting go of a bad attitude. He smiled tightly. "You get a kick out of being a smartass, don't you?"

She shrugged. "Maybe."

"Uh-huh. That'll fizzle out quickly." Without missing a beat, the major returned his attention to the contract in the folder and continued as if their exchange was like a normal conversation. "I'll give you the short version anyway. This is your contract with the United States Army and, specifically, with the Oriceran Integration Program, operating under one of the 307th Combat Battalion's Special Operations units. *My* unit.

"When you sign your name on every single dotted line in front of you, you sign your life over to me. I'm your superior, your commander, your boss. I am *not* your mama.

We'll put you through the program's specialized training, which is—"

"Bootcamp for magicals," Carmine interjected.

Winters held his breath, then let it out in a sigh. "Something like that. Until you've finished that specialized training, you will eat, sleep, breathe, and shit where we tell you. Same thing applies on a general scale after that, with a few minor changes depending on where I station y'all next in whatever MOS I select."

When the pixies gave him blank stares in response, he added, "Complete bootcamp, then you get your jobs. Any questions?"

The room was silent for a moment, then Domino nodded. "Yeah. Why's the gnome here?"

"Because so far," Carmine answered instead, "Major Winters' been lucky enough never to have struck a deal with *one* pixie, let alone three. Unfortunately, *I* have."

Z choked back a laugh. "So, you're here to make sure we put down the right names when we sign, huh?"

The gnome didn't react to her blatant admission of how tricky pixies could be. He deadpanned, "I don't give a shit what name you put down."

Winters looked at him in surprise, then frowned. "That's not—"

"Uh-huh." Carmine held up a clawed hand to stop the man from saying anything else while looking from one pixie face to the next. He spun his walking stick in his hand as he continued. "Names change. Promises get broken. Handshakes and smiles aren't enough sometimes."

He nodded at the stacks of paper in front of each pixie. "*I'm* here to get rid of the loopholes."

Z and her cousins exchanged confused glances for show. She raised an eyebrow at the contract meant for her, then flashed the old gnome a smirk. "By reading the whole thing out loud and changing around a few words, or…"

"That could be fun," Domino added.

Winters closed his eyes.

Carmine tilted his head as if he were considering that. "For most folks, a legally binding contract is enough to keep 'em in line. If they don't *stay* in line, it makes sure they suffer the agreed consequences. However, a legally binding contract ain't gonna make three lawless pixies follow the rules, is it?"

Z and Domino kept their mouths shut. Echo produced a devious grin that made the major frown in concern.

"*That's* why I'm here," the gnome continued. The top of his walking stick glowed. "To make sure you sign those contracts with something stronger than ink."

The pixies exchanged knowing looks, then Domino wiggled his eyebrows. "He's talking about blood, right? That sounds like even *more* fun."

"Oh, *boy*." Z let her smile match the intensity of Echo's grin and widened her eyes at Major Winters. "You mean we get to sign our names in our blood? You couldn't have known, Major, but that made my cousin's day."

Echo rubbed her hands together in excitement and kept grinning at their boss-to-be.

"Shit." Domino wrinkled his nose and slumped in his chair. "I left my ritual dagger back in the rotting log. That thing was sharp, too, lemme tell ya. You got anything pokey on you, Z?"

She patted herself down, then spread her arms. "Fresh out, man. My bad."

They both turned to the right and chorused, "Echo?"

The goth pixie wiggled her eyebrows.

The major studied their faces and shook his head, maintaining a straight face. "I am not letting y'all within twenty feet of a sharp object."

Domino looked baffled by the revelation. "Then how are we supposed to sign on the dotted line, Major? Unless, I mean, do you already have a cut, and you're offering *yours* instead?"

Carmine cracked the butt of his stick on the tile floor, and the tip flashed. "Pull your shit together so we can get this over with. You're backing up my schedule."

Z lifted both hands in concession and sat back in her chair. "Shit, Mr. Mediator. My bad."

Domino leaned forward with a concerned look. "I heard Ex-Lax works really well for that."

Z nodded. "You need more fiber in your diet, gnome. That's what everybody's saying. Major, can we get him some fiber?"

Echo snorted and glanced at the gnome.

To their credit, neither the major nor the gnome took their banter to heart. Major Winters waited until Echo had stopped snickering, then asked, "Y'all done?"

"They are." Electric-blue light flared from the tip of Carmine's walking stick in an obvious warning as he glared at the pixies. "Hand 'em those pens, Major. They're ready to sign."

CHAPTER THIRTEEN

Z and her cousins could talk shit with the best of them, and if Carmine Ratchetter hadn't been there to turn their Army contracts into something stronger than *legally* binding, the pixies would have attempted an escape. They would've played nice until the perfect moment presented itself for them to leave.

That was why the old gnome hadn't left. He'd maintained his mediator status long enough to sit in on this final meeting and make sure the Army's new magical recruits couldn't weasel out of the deal. It was clear that he *did* know pixies, and he understood these three very well.

When Winters handed pens to his recruits, the blue light at the top of Carmine's staff got brighter and didn't fade. The major walked them through the process as Z and her cousins flipped through the contracts' pages. "Everywhere there's a dotted line. Initials. Signature. Whatever it asks for. Let's make sure you get them all the first time."

Z found the first signature line beside the date and time and scoffed as she started to form a big Z in black ink. Half a second after the ink flowed onto the paper, blue light traced the signature she'd penned.

On either side of her, that light glowed on the pages Domino and Echo were in the middle of signing.

When she looked at the gnome, he was wearing a crooked smile that was not friendly.

She smirked. "Neat trick."

"That's just the first page."

Z returned her attention to the contract and flipped to the next page.

Smart gnome, she thought. *Binding us to this stupid deal with magical signatures. Did he enchant the contract or the pens?*

Z didn't bother reading anything in the contract after that since there was no point. Looking for loopholes was useless. Searching for anything she could argue about to preserve freedom a little longer wouldn't make a difference. She and her cousins would have to figure everything out through trial and error since the contract didn't cover the terms in enough detail to prepare the pixies for what they'd experience in the months to come.

This had been their choice, though, so they had to deal with it.

We get to stay on Earth. That's all that matters, Z told herself.

Major Winters looked surprised by the speed with which she turned the pages and scribbled Z on every dotted line. Her cousins moved through the process more slowly, but she was sure neither was paying attention to the words on the pages. Having the blue light appear after every pen stroke held their attention.

"What exactly does that do?" Domino asked without

looking up from yet another page. "The magical part."

"Insurance to keep you all in line," Carmine muttered in response. "And to keep you from digging an even deeper hole for yourselves while you wait."

"For what?" Z asked.

The gnome's expression was impassive. "If any of you fucks up enough that it counts as trying to break your contract, I'll know it."

"Great." She rolled her eyes and signed another page.

"Try to run or skip out, I'll know," he continued. "Get into enough trouble, I'll know. Use your magic in a way you're not supposed to, I'll know."

Winters cleared his throat and muttered, "You can't get rid of their magic altogether?"

Carmine scoffed, slammed the butt of his stick on the floor, and spun to face the major. "I *could*, but what the hell's the point of an Oriceran Integration Program if the Oricerans are as magic-less as the rest of you?"

The major stared at the consultant, then shrugged and went back to looking at the sample contract. "Never mind."

Carmine shook his head and kept talking like he hadn't been interrupted by the question. "Contrary to popular belief, I got shit to take care of in other parts of the country. If I find out that the Army's three magical *amigos* screwed up bad enough to get my attention, kiss your temporary freedom goodbye, starting with being locked in this room again for however long it takes me to finish what I'm doing elsewhere."

The gnome looked at each pixie in turn, then snickered. "Or for however long I feel like making you wait. Want me to write that down?"

Z clicked her tongue. "We're signing the damn thing, aren't we?"

"Sure. Doesn't mean shit 'til we get to the end."

The pixies finished signing and initialing their contract packets in tense silence. While she signed with black ink that was traced with Carmine's magical blue, Z couldn't stop thinking about the specific way the old gnome had laid out the parameters.

Only if we screw up badly enough to get his attention, huh? I guess signing on three pixies with zero other options and expecting them to behave like regular soldiers is asking for a little too much. There's some wiggle room.

Once the gnome was out of their hair and on his way back to wherever he came from, she and her cousins could test how much wiggle room this new Oriceran Integration Program allowed.

When Domino and Echo reached the final page of their contracts, Major Winters cleared his throat. "Final two pieces of the process. Sign your full name at the very bottom, then hand it to me. I'll do the same."

Z didn't understand why he felt like he had to say that out loud when it was written at the bottom of the final page, but she put pen to paper and wrote her full name in black. Glowing electric blue traced the lines.

Probably likes to hear himself talk. Makes him feel like he's got this all under control. Otherwise, he'd spend too much time thinking about how little control he'll have over three pixies. Should've thought of that before he offered us this deal.

"All right. Give 'em here." Winters gestured, and the pixies sent the stacks over. The contracts spun and slid toward him, and he managed to sweep them up into a chaotic jumble before any of the papers hit the floor.

Before situating the paperwork again, he glared at the pixies, but what could he do? They were signing their lives away to the Army, and specifically to his program. If he wanted obedient new guinea pigs, he shouldn't have recruited pixies.

"All right. First up is Domino Thornbrook. Domino? Are you serious?"

Domino raised his eyebrows. "Like the game, not the pizza. I heard the game's way more fun."

Winters turned to Carmine. "Is he fucking with me?"

"Probably not."

"'Domino?'"

"Hey, man! Saying my name three times isn't gonna change it."

The major glowered at him, then grunted in frustration. He pulled a smartphone out of his pocket and scrolled through his apps to the one he wanted. Then he set the phone on the table, picked up his pen, and held it above where he would sign.

"Last part is on the record, meaning I'm recording y'all now. This covers my ass as much as yours. So. Domino Thornbrook…" He grimaced as he said the name like he had difficulty getting his mouth to form the appropriate shapes for the right sounds, then cleared his throat. "Do you willingly agree to participate in the United States Army's experimental Oriceran Integration Program, otherwise referred to as the OIP, as an Army soldier for the duration of the program and potentially longer?"

Domino shot Z a quick glance, then flashed the major a

crooked smile. "Sure."

"Say 'yes,'" Winters hissed. "So it doesn't require interpretation."

"Okay."

The major opened his mouth to correct the pixie, but Carmine stopped him by grumbling, "I think that's as good as you're gonna get."

"Jesus Christ," Winters whispered, but he perked up and continued the recorded swearing-in of the three Oriceran magicals. "Do you understand that this contract remains in effect beyond a potential dissolution of the OIP until your honorable or dishonorable discharge or command-approved retirement from the United States Army?"

"Uh-huh."

The major looked like he wanted to reach over the table and punch Domino in the face. Instead, he tapped his pen on the table, then flipped the packet around and added his signature at the bottom of the last page. After that, he organized the pile of paperwork in front of him. "Next is…Z?"

"Present." Z raised her hand and gave him a sickly-sweet grin.

"Nope. We don't use just a letter on official documents." He tossed Z's contract back across the table and pointed at the signature. "You need to put your full name on the line."

She slapped a hand on the contract, met the major's gaze, and slid it back to him in a flurry of skittering papers. "That *is* my real name."

Winters scoffed. "Bullshit."

"You wanna talk about bullshit?"

"Uh-oh," Domino muttered, sinking down in his chair.

Z lurched to her feet and slapped both hands on the

table this time, then leaned threateningly toward her new boss. "How about forcing us into this pathetic game of yours? *That's* bullshit."

Shaking his head, Domino commented, "Shouldn't've said anything about her name."

"How about, I have no idea how long we've been in this room, but we were probably here in an unofficial and *illegal* capacity. More bullshit. If you wanna get technical—"

"Take a seat," Winters ordered, but she didn't listen. Z was just getting started.

"You whipped up a program it looks like you don't even want. You've recruited magicals for it who wanna go back to Oriceran only *slightly* less than they want to work for you. Now you assume that because human names have more than one letter, a fucking pixie from a different planet doesn't have a real first name that's just Z!"

She ended her diatribe with widespread arms and an echoing shout that made even Carmine flinch. That was because she'd all but climbed onto the tabletop to emphasize her point.

Nobody moved or said a word after she finished. Then Major Winters lifted his chin, held Z's enraged gaze, and swallowed. "Take a seat so we can continue."

Z nodded at the messy contract on the table. "As soon as you put your signature under Z Thornbrook."

She knew this wasn't the best way to kick off her future working relationship with the man, but that awareness was a weak, quiet voice compared to her rage. During her long life, Z had learned to ride the wave of that rage since that was the only way to keep from imploding.

She wasn't going to back down from this one, magic or no magic.

Winters licked his lips. "Is that how you want to handle this? Right off the bat?"

"Major," Carmine stated as he leaned toward the officer, though his dark, beady eyes remained on the blue-haired pixie who was breathing heavily on the table. "I suggest you pick your battles with this one. *Very* carefully."

The gnome's warning made more of an impression on the human than anything Z had said so far. Winters shot Carmine a glance of defiant disbelief, then growled and picked up the last page of Z's contract. "All right. Z Thornbrook. Do you willingly agree to participate in the United States Army's experimental Oriceran Integration Program, otherwise referred to as the OIP, as a registered Army soldier for the duration of the program and potentially longer?"

"Uh-huh." It wasn't a "yes," but Z didn't want to run the risk of having another tantrum. She stared at the major as he continued with his prepared script, which required verbal assent, and answered each question in the affirmative.

When Winters had finished adding his signature to the bottom of her contract, Z went back to her seat.

He gazed at her, then raised his eyebrows. "Good to see that you're a pixie of your word."

Carmine didn't remind the major that he was treading on thin ice. Instead, the gnome clicked his tongue and stroked his hairless, wrinkled chin to keep from spouting more wry comments that had the potential to make *him* the target of Z's anger.

She noticed. *They think we're a joke, but they're smart enough to be scared. If they didn't need us for this program, none of us would be sitting here right now.*

Winters went through Echo's contract to make sure she'd signed everything. He seemed surprised to find everything in perfect order, and though Echo's name was also strange, it contained more than one letter.

"Here we go, then," he began. "Echo Thornbrook, do you agree to participate in the United States Army's experimental Oriceran Integration Program, otherwise referred to as the OIP, as a registered Army soldier for the duration of the program and potentially longer?"

When she didn't reply, the major raised his eyebrows.

Echo gave him two thumbs-up and nodded.

He sighed. "Apparently, I didn't make this clear. I need verbal confirmation."

She shrugged, gestured at her contract, and gave him two thumbs-up again.

Winters stared at her for a moment, then looked to Z and Domino for answers. "What's wrong with her?"

"Whoa, whoa, hey." Domino lifted his hands and growled, "How about we *don't* jump to conclusions, huh?"

"There's nothing wrong with her," Z added blandly.

The major looked confused but returned his attention to Echo. "Then let's try this again. Echo Thornbrook, do you willingly agree…"

The goth pixie gave him two thumbs-up with a hefty dose of sarcasm and zero words.

"You have to be kidding me," he grumbled. "Does she talk?"

Domino leaned back in his chair and folded his arms.

"Not to *you*."

Winters closed his eyes and pinched the bridge of his nose between thumb and forefinger.

Carmine cleared his throat. "Let the record show that one Echo Thornbrook, who is joining the OIP, has, in the absence of verbal confirmation, provided visual confirmation of understanding and has willingly entered this agreement with the US Army."

The major's eyes flew open, and he stared at the gnome. "Sign the damn contract, Major."

Whether Carmine's command held sufficient warning or Major Winters was at the end of his rope, he bit his lower lip and scribbled his John Hancock on the line below Echo's signature.

The second he finished, Carmine leaned toward the still-recording cellphone and stated, "There you have it, folks. Signed, sealed, and delivered." He stabbed a crooked finger at the phone's screen to stop the recording.

As he struggled to get to his feet, using his walking stick as both support and leverage, Winters grabbed his phone, saw that his consultant had ended the recording, and scowled at the stiff, grunting gnome. "What are you doing?"

"You got what you wanted, Major. The contracts are signed. The magic's in place. They're yours now, for better or worse. They're in, and I'm gettin' the hell outta here." Without waiting for a response, Carmine shoved his chair back and shuffled toward the door.

Major Winters studied the pixies, then stood and headed after his consultant. "Hold on a second. I was under the impression that you'd stick around to see this through."

"I did. Business completed."

"You expect me to take it from here on my own?"

With an exasperated sigh, Carmine stopped and faced the major. "Hate to burst your damn bubble, Major, but you're not the only person, human or magical, who's begging for my help with touchy situations. I helped you get this far. The rest is on you and your men. And women. Or whatever."

"Fine," Winters snapped. "What happens if I need to reach you?"

"You can't." When the major looked baffled, Carmine rolled his eyes. "If it gets bad enough that you need me, I'll find you. If I don't show up, you don't really need me."

"It'd be easier if you—"

Before the major could finish his sentence, Carmine slammed the butt of his walking stick on the floor. Light flared at the tip with such blinding intensity that one human and three pixies had to turn away to shield their eyes. When the glare faded, the gnome was gone.

Winters looked angry.

Domino snickered. "Looks like it's just us, Major."

Z gave her new boss a crooked smile. "This'll be fun."

"Unless I ask you a question and expect an immediate answer, I don't want to hear another word from any of you." Winters stormed back to the table to collect the signed contracts. His frown deepened, and when he glanced at them, he seemed to have a hard time deciding which he wanted to focus on first. "The gnome didn't tell me much about you other than where we could find you and that some of you might choose the OIP over getting shipped to a different planet."

Z tried not to laugh in the major's face. "Come on. It's not like you're doing this out of the goodness of your heart. What else do you wanna know?"

"Thornbrook," Winters murmured.

Domino shot him a conspiratorial wink. "That's the name, man. Don't wear it out."

The major looked at the pixies blankly and shook his head. "So, what? You're siblings?"

"Ha!" Domino pointed at himself and his sister. "Just me and Echo."

He settled his gaze on Z. "Great. Don't tell me you're their mom."

She forced out a laugh. "Fuck you."

"Not like it's any of your business," Domino cut in. "But her dad and our mom came from the same union if you know what I'm sayin'."

The major raised an eyebrow and held Z's fiery gaze. "You're cousins."

She plastered a fake smile on her lips. "Check it out. The major knows how family trees work."

"Most humans have sixth-grade biology class to thank for that." Their boss looked at all three pixies. "Time to put you to work. Let's move."

He didn't slow down to wait for them, nor did he turn around to make sure his three new soldiers realized that meant they were being let out.

Z rose to her feet, sighed, and nodded for her cousins to join her in following Major Winters.

No one said life on Earth was gonna be easy. Even this shit-show is a hell of a lot easier than going back to Oriceran. We'll make the most of it while we can.

CHAPTER FOURTEEN

Over the next six hours, Z and her cousins went through the unorthodox process of Army intake for magical recruits, which was chaotic, messy, and embarrassing for the humans involved because it was the first time any of them had had to deviate from the usual process. Also because they were dealing with pixies instead of humans.

Z and her cousins didn't make it easy on them.

When they stepped out of the holding room to follow Major Winters, Z's legs almost gave out when her magic surged back to her all at once. When she realized she had full access to her magic, it took only seconds to go from a normal-looking woman who was five-foot-five to two inches of glowing blue light and glittering wings.

It was almost as intoxicating as combining the magic of a dozen pixies to shrink their stolen goods.

The same sensations rushed through Domino and Echo, and their joy was obvious as well. Echo let out a childlike giggle. Her brother stumbled sideways until his shoulder thumped the wall, and he dreamily uttered, "Whoa, dude."

Major Winters turned around to see only two of his new recruits behind him when there should have been three. Both of them looked like they'd spent the last twenty-four hours at a bar instead of more or less *behind* bars.

"What is wrong with you?" he snapped as he searched the hallway. "And where's the other one? X, or Y, or…"

"Z, Major," Z corrected as she zipped toward him from the ceiling. "It's the last letter of the alphabet. Shouldn't be *that* hard to remember."

Winters tensed when he heard the abnormally high-pitched voice and spun to search for the source of it. It took him a moment to realize that the orb of blue light hovering ahead of him was his third recruit. Domino and Echo filled the hall with titters.

He glowered at Z and breathed heavily through his nose. "You're out of line, pixie."

"Really?" Hovering a few feet from his face, she folded her arms and smirked at the giant human. "Nobody said anything about forming a line."

"And nobody gave you permission to do *that*." He fluttered a hand at her, not capable of saying she'd shrunk to her natural size and looked like a sparkly, human-shaped butterfly. "So cut that out."

"Aw, come on, Major." Z zipped across the hall, made a quick loop in the air, then stopped to raise both arms and sighed. "We've been cooped up *forever*. Can't a pixie get a minute to stretch her wings?"

"No," Winters barked. "Now, go normal. That's an order."

Rolling her eyes, she dropped her arms to her sides and changed back.

Even though growing to human size was what the major had told her to do, he took a step back when the two-inch tall blue orb ballooned into a five-foot-five woman again. The blue wings stayed.

"No. Uh-uh." Winters vehemently shook his head. "That's not part of the—"

"Oh, *shit*, this feels good," Domino exclaimed as he stretched his arms to the sides. The shimmering brown wings that sprouted from his human-looking back unfurled, and he fluttered them in satisfaction.

Echo's wings were as black as the rest of her ensemble. With a dreamy, half-drunk smile curling her lips, she folded her arms and closed her eyes, reveling in having her pixie appendages and the full use of her magic.

"That wasn't part of the deal," the major grumbled as he stabbed a finger at the siblings.

Domino tried to push away from the wall and swayed from the intoxicating strength of his magic, then slumped against the wall with a giggle. "What's that?"

"All that fairy—" Winters was interrupted by Domino and Echo gasping in surprise and wearing nearly identical expressions of insult. The major glared at them and spread his arms. "What?"

"We don't use the F-word," Z explained.

"Right?" Domino chuckled and shook his head. "Fuck that."

"If you have to call us something," she continued, "stick with pixies."

Echo leaned toward her brother to whisper in his ear.

"She says we'll give you a free pass," Domino translated. "Just this once."

"For the love of—" Winters clenched his fists at his sides, glaring at the magic-drunk siblings while a vein popped out on his temple. "I don't care what y'all wanna be called. You're not walking around this facility with *wings* on your backs. This is the Army, not the circus."

"You're the one who wanted pixies in your program, Major," Z countered.

He spun to face her, looking like he was about to burst a few blood vessels.

Failing to hide a smirk, Z lifted her hands. "We're pixies. Not something you see in every circus, but it's occurred to me how cool it would be to join one."

"Stop talking." Winters had plumbed the depths of his willpower to regain his self-control, and his scowl disappeared beneath a mask of tough apathy. He looked over his shoulder at Domino and Echo, who were gazing dreamily at each other. "What's their deal?"

"We're out of the cage, so our magic's back," Z replied, then clicked her tongue. "Think of it like standing up too fast and liking the feeling, only it lasts longer."

"How long?" he snapped.

"How should I know? We've never been locked up for that long."

"Come on." Major Winters stormed past her down the hall, leaving a trail of angry, echoing footsteps behind him. "No flying. No shrinking. No tricks. Got it?"

"Uh-huh." Z caught her cousins' attention and nodded for them to follow her and their new boss. Domino shot her the guns with both hands and grinned like a lunatic. Echo spun in a staggering circle and stretched her wings like a little girl twirling in a new dress. The three pixies were off to start their new careers, feeling like their true selves.

Unfortunately, the Army personnel assigned to facilitate the intake of the new recruits didn't appreciate the pixies' true selves. It took the bored corporal behind the desk a full sixty seconds to stop staring at the three recruits with *wings* strutting through the open room behind Major Winters. Even when the major stopped in front of the desk and gave him orders to process three new soldiers into the OIP, the corporal was slow to reply.

"If you can't snap out of it, Corporal Packard, I wonder if a week of filing paperwork at the HHC might do it," Winters warned.

"Ooh." Rubbing his hands together, Domino nodded. "I'd like to see *that*."

The major ignored the ridiculous comment from behind him and Corporal Packard's surprise. "Is that going to be necessary?"

"No, Major." Blinking, the stunned corporal finally managed to pull his gaze away from the black, copper, and deep blue wings sprouting from the backs of the three human-looking beings and looked at the paperwork on the desktop. "We're ready to start."

The United States Army *wasn't* ready to enter three magicals into the regular system. The first sign of difficulty came when the pixies were ushered to the station with digital scanners to add their fingerprints to the Army's system.

After attempting to take Z's fingerprints, Corporal Packard was on the verge of bolting. "Um, Major Winters?"

Narrowing his eyes, the major looked up from the folding metal chair he'd appropriated to get comfortable with an Army-approved magazine. "Try resetting the scanner, Corporal."

"It's not that, sir." Packard waved his CO toward him. "You might wanna take a look at this."

The major rose laboriously from the chair and came toward them.

Domino leaned toward Z to mutter, "Five bucks says the bull snorts smoke out of his nose by the end of the day."

Echo hissed a laugh and shook her head.

Z shot her cousins a playful frown. "You don't have five bucks."

"Fine. What are we betting with, then?"

"You have a private stash of valuables somewhere? In case you forgot, everything we owned got blasted to smithereens by a bunch of useless—"

"What is it?" Winters interrupted when he reached the station with the fingerprint scanner, which was connected to a clunky-looking laptop.

Corporal Packard ignored the weirdness of the conversation he'd overheard and focused on his job, which was just as weird. "There's, uh… Well, there's something wrong with her fingerprints."

He turned the laptop toward the major and waited.

Winters frowned at the image on the screen, then turned the same expression on Z. "What part of 'hold still for the scanner' don't you get?"

She shot him a crooked smile. "If that's Army code, all of it."

"It's not the new recruit, Major," Packard added, "Or the scanner. There's no malfunction. I think that is her actual fingerprint."

Winters turned a blank stare on the corporal. "What about it?"

"It…keeps moving." Packard let out a defeated sigh and shook his head. "When I did another scan, the image came up blurry again."

"He redid it three times," Z added helpfully.

"I said no tricks," Winters growled.

"No tricks. Honest." She held up her hands, shoved one closer to the major's face, and grinned. "Just pixies being pixies."

Winters leaned away from her hand, and his scowl deepened when he realized that the pads of her fingers and her palm were swirling, which made fingerprinting impossible. "Why didn't you say anything about this?"

Z shrugged. "I'm not going to tell you how to do your job."

"That's rude," Domino added. "What do you think we are, Major? Dictators?"

"I…" Winters blinked, then dipped his head to pinch the bridge of his nose. "Skip the fingerprinting for now, Corporal Packard."

"Sure." The corporal looked at the three smiling pixies

and his frustrated commanding officer. "That removes the next few steps of processing, Major. Can't create ID cards or security clearance until their fingerprints are in the system."

"I know how it works."

"Right." Quirking his lips, Packard continued to gaze at his CO. Winters was deeply entrenched in staving off a migraine and trying to calm down. "Major?"

"What?"

"What do you want me to do with them next?"

Taking a long, slow breath, Winters opened his eyes and stared blankly at the corporal. The newly promoted soldier had shown administrative promise, and a newly formed unit was the best place for him to cut his teeth on his new rank. "Whatever doesn't rely on them being in the system, Corporal."

"Yes, sir." Nodding, Packard sidestepped out from behind the station, casting the pixies wary glances as he moved. "Just, uh, follow me."

Domino turned the major and put both hands on his hips. "Permission to do what your lackey says, Major?"

"His *what*?" Packard echoed, his expression a mix of disbelief and disgust.

Winters didn't immediately answer the question. In his mind, he heard Carmine telling him that three pixies in his new program were three too many and to pick his battles.

"You don't need permission to follow orders from another of your superiors," he stated. "Corporal Packard has earned his rank and the right to be addressed by it. If I hear you call him anything but corporal, we will have problems."

Domino forced his expression into a business-like scowl that matched the major's. "Aye aye, Cap'n. Major. Captain Major?"

Jesus fucking Christ. Winters nodded at Packard. "Uniforms. Bedding. Then drop 'em off at the barracks."

The corporal glanced at the pixies, leaned toward his CO, and dropped his voice to barely above a whisper. "Just to make sure, you're talking about the temporary bay here, not the real barracks, right?"

"That's correct, Corporal." Winters clapped a hand on Packard's shoulder in a poor attempt at reassurance. "Don't let 'em get to you and you'll be fine." He headed toward the other side of the room. Alone.

Packard looked like he wanted to scuttle after his superior, but he held his ground. "Where are you going, sir?"

"To see if anyone has anything stronger than Tylenol to take the edge off my migraine. I'll find you later. They're yours 'til then." The major didn't slow his gait as he marched swiftly across the room toward the far door.

Packard swallowed but managed to pull himself together as he turned back to the three pixies who were now *his* responsibility. "Let's, uh...let's go."

Domino spread his arms and eyed the corporal. "If you're *sure*..."

"You look scared, Corporal," Z added with a concerned frown. "Anything we can do to help you feel more comfortable?"

"Yeah. Stop talking." He glared at the three of them. "And get rid of those things."

"What things?" Domino asked, feigning cluelessness.

"Your wings."

"Wings?" Z gaped at the corporal like he'd insulted her intelligence.

Echo spun in a slow circle, looking over her shoulder at her black wings like a dog chasing its tail. She fluttered them and snorted.

Domino pointed at his sister. "You mean *those* wings?"

"Why didn't you just say so?" Z wagged a finger at the young soldier and smiled. "Sorry, but no can do, Corporal. Those are part of the package."

Packard stared blankly at them, then a frown creased his brow. "Just shut up and follow me."

"Aye aye!" Domino called after him. He leaned toward Z again. "Do we call a corporal Cap'n too?"

"As much as we call a major Cap'n."

Echo whispered in her brother's ear. "She says more like a major buzzkill."

The pixies cracked up as they followed Packard out of the room, and the corporal called on every iota of his willpower to keep from fleeing. He muttered, "I shouldn't have signed up for this."

Outfitting the three with standard-issue Army uniforms would have been the least frustrating part of the intake process if the pixies hadn't used Major Winters' absence as an opportunity to find out how much they could get away with.

Packard didn't have anyone else in the supply room to back him up while he searched for properly sized pants, shirts, undergarments, and boots.

"Hey, Corporal? What's this?"

"That is a radio. Put it down."

"Radio, huh? Where's the music? Every channel's blank."

"Not that kind. No. *No*. Quit touching buttons. That's a satellite GPS, not a videogame."

"Sure looks like one."

"Corporal, how long's this sandwich been here? It *is* a sandwich, right?"

"Hey, gimme a bite of that. I'm hungry too."

"*You* ate your dinner. This thing can't be older than... What do you think, Corporal? Four days? It's more appetizing than the slop on those trays was."

"Share."

"No. Find your own four-day-old sandwich. Finders keepers, man."

"Z. Seriously. I want a sandwich."

"Yeah? How bad do you want it? You're gonna have to take it from me."

"All three of you, shut the fuck up!" Packard roared.

The storage room fell silent. He straightened from the plastic crate of uniforms and turned to face the pixies. He'd intended to tell them to sit down, touch nothing, and not say another word, but their expressions made a tight knot form in his gut.

Z and Domino gazed at Echo and Corporal Packard. Z's lips were pursed, and Domino tried to hide his grimace with a hand that didn't quite cover it.

Echo stood in the center of the room with her arms folded, glaring at the corporal with a level of hatred he had never experienced.

One black combat boot tapped the tile floor, the only sound in the silence. The most terrifying part was that her pitch-black wings were stretched to their fullest span but perfectly still.

It reminded Corporal Packard of a hunting dog's tail when it caught its quarry's scent or the hood of a cobra flaring as the creature coiled to strike.

"What—" His voice cracked, so he cleared his throat and tried again. "What's her deal?"

Domino replied. "You can't tell?"

Z nodded. "She's pissed, Corporal."

"Right. Well, this… This is the Army. Everybody gets yelled at, and everybody's pissed. If any of you can't handle it—"

"If *you're* gonna tell us to shut the fuck up," Z interrupted, "you should address the right pixies."

Corporal Packard scrunched his face in bafflement. "*What?*"

Domino shrugged. "You said all three of us. My sister found that insulting."

"Why the fuck would—"

"She doesn't talk, Corporal."

Nodding, Z shot the stunned human a wink. "Leave her out of it, huh?"

"Out of *what*? We're not *in* anything. The only thing that's happening right now is that *I* have orders to get uniforms on you morons. Now *you* have orders to let me do my fucking job."

"Ooh." Z turned to Domino with a playful grimace. "*Somebody's* touchy."

"Maybe Corporal Packard needs some help lightening up."

"No." He pointed at them. "I don't need help with anything, and not from—"

"Come on, man. We can totally help."

"Pixies are *great* at helping."

"We're the best."

Before Packard could shout at them again, which he would have, the angry goth pixie disappeared in a flicker of dark light. That wiped everything else from his mind. She reappeared in front of his face, only two inches tall, with a tight, fake closed-lipped smile on her face.

The corporal's Army training and exercise drills had not prepared him for having a two-inch-tall person with wings inside his personal space. Frozen in indecision, Packard managed to take a quick breath.

Echo shot him a disapproving frown, then zipped forward, placed a hand on each corner of his mouth, and shoved up with both hands to get him to smile.

Corporal Packard reeled away from her with a squeal.

Z and Domino burst out laughing.

"Now, *that's* a smile."

"Don't quit now, Corporal. You are doing so well!"

"Don't humans say something about laughter being the best medicine?"

"If it is, Corporal Packard must be *really* sick."

While the corporal recovered from having a pixie touch his mouth, Echo zipped behind him to dive head-first into the crate of uniforms. Before he knew what was happening, articles of clothing were sailing over his head from behind him while Z and Domino played Catch the Clothing."

"Wow. They don't give a shit about style, do they?"

"*This* is kinda cool. What is it, a smock?"

"Ha! Do you even know what a smock is?"

"Meh. Oh, damn. This one's *huge*. Hey, Corporal. Does the Army have, like, a cutoff for how big a human soldier can be? What if some guy was seven feet tall and had a chest like a boulder? Would you guys have to pay for a personal tailor?"

"Find anything in there for *you*, Echo? No? That's fine. We can work with what we've got."

Corporal Packard was unable to move as the magical recruits trashed the storage room and removed most of the uniforms from the plastic bin. One thought kept circling through his mind.

There goes my career.

He partially snapped out of it when Z's mad-looking grin appeared in his face. She cheerfully asked, "Hey, Corporal. These uniforms are great and all, but they need a few modifications. You got any scissors in here?"

Packard swallowed hard, took a gasping breath, and backed up against the wall. He slid down it to the floor.

"That's okay." Z joined her cousins in going through everything in the supply room. "We'll figure it out."

CHAPTER FIFTEEN

Two hours later, Z and her cousins were alone in another room. This one was much bigger and was not locked. It contained half a dozen metal bunk beds, each with a metal drawer for personal belongings beneath the bottom bunk. Since only three of Major Winters' potential recruits had chosen to sign up, each pixie had claimed two bunk beds, which they pushed together to make a three-bunk circle in the center of the room.

Z lay on her double-wide bottom bunk with her hands behind her head and one ankle crossed over the opposite knee, bouncing her foot. "I don't know, guys. This is turning out to be anticlimactic."

"Corporal Packard looked like he was having fun," Domino countered.

They chuckled when they remembered how long it had taken the corporal to come out of his catatonic state before he was able to take them to what he called "the bay."

"Yep." Z let out a contented sigh. "So much fun that he

ran out of here to get to his own bed, right? He just can't wait to start all over again tomorrow."

"At least he stopped talking," Echo muttered. She rolled onto her side to face the center of the bunk circle. "Maybe he's the only soldier we'll ever see while we're in training. But then, what if something happens to him? What if he gets sick? Or dies? Will we have to go through this whole thing again like we did today?"

Domino snorted. "I don't think Packard's the program, Echo."

"Maybe you're right." She propped her head up on one hand and sighed. "It didn't look like he knew what he was doing. That kinda makes me wonder how many humans with half a brain they keep stocked in this place."

"Stocked?" Z laughed. "We're taking orders from a bunch of nonperishable food items now?"

"You know what?" Domino fluffed his pillow. "A jar of peanut butter would probably get more done in a day."

His sister pointed at him. "*Crunchy* peanut butter."

"Of course."

"So far," Z added, glancing at her cousins and trying not to look concerned about their answer, "you guys don't wish we'd just shipped off to Oriceran instead, right?"

The siblings stopped smiling and stared at her in silence.

Echo shook her head. "Don't ever say that again."

"I didn't think humans were contagious," Domino added, "but I'm starting to wonder. You feelin' okay, Z?"

She flashed them a smile, then rolled her head across her pillow to stare at the underside of the bunk above her. "Just trying to keep you guys on your toes."

Echo scoffed. "Well, check our toes without going somewhere so dark and terrifying next time, huh?"

"Says the pixie whose first thought about everything goes straight to death and dismemberment."

"We weren't talking about death and dismemberment, but now that you brought it up…"

The goth didn't have time to dive into her favorite conversational topic because the bay's squeaky metal door flew open with a bang, and in walked Major Winters.

The man looked like he'd been ready to storm into the room and break up a fistfight, so it took him a few seconds to realize there was no bedlam or chaos, only three pixies lying on their beds. It didn't seem like they'd done anything more than rearrange the furniture.

Domino grinned and sat up on the edge of his bunk. "*There's* our favorite guy!"

Z wiggled her fingers at him but didn't get up from her comfortable prone position. "Hi, Major."

Winters swept his gaze across the bay, then scowled at the pixies. "What the hell are you doing?"

"Nothing." Z gestured at the furniture. "Literally."

"I think Corporal Packard might be sick, though," Domino added. "He was sweaty and gray-looking in the face when he dropped us off here and said not to go anywhere. Then he took off without even saying goodnight. Maybe you should go check on him."

Z and Echo nodded silently to back him up, each wearing her version of nonauthentic concern.

Winters pressed his lips together. "I did. Right before he told me he didn't think he could continue serving in his current capacity and do his job effectively. Corporal

Packard's never been deployed, but he looks like he just got back from a tour of hell. What happened?"

Z and her cousins exchanged curious gazes. Then she pushed up off the thin mattress to sit on the edge of her bunk. "We didn't touch him, Major. Honest."

"Well." Domino shrugged and pointed at his sister. "*She* did."

Echo's jaw dropped as she stared at him in disbelief.

"We were trying to get him to lighten up," Z explained. "Everyone around here's so freakin' serious, you know?"

Winters folded his arms. "Both Army personnel you've interacted with since signing on?"

"Yeah." Domino looked like he was going to stand and head toward the officer. "Hey, maybe *you* should try smiling more."

"Don't touch me." Winters pointed at him with a harsh enough warning in his eyes that the pixie sat back on his bunk, provoking a series of protesting squeaks from the old metal frame.

That didn't stop Domino from chuckling.

Another moment of silence passed, then Z popped her lips since the quiet was getting to her. "So, what now?"

"Now?" Winters scanned the bay again as if he couldn't believe that three pixies who had been left on their own had *not* started trouble. He couldn't find any proof of said trouble, so there was nothing more to say. "Now it's lights out."

"Oh, okay." Domino grinned. "So, the Army's just, like, a giant babysitter."

"With guns," Z added, wiggling her eyebrows at her cousin. "Who lets you *play* with them."

"Oh, trust me." For the first time since they'd met him, the major laughed. "I'm not letting y'all anywhere near the firearms, even without live rounds. Now shut up and go to sleep. When I come back at oh five hundred, I better see all y'all in uniform and with every one of those bunks crisply made up."

He turned on his heel and stormed out of the bay. The door thunked shut behind him, and the pixies were left to their own devices.

"That was amazing," Domino murmured as he stared at the closed door.

"What was?"

As he turned his head to meet Z's gaze, a loud click echoed through the bay, and the overhead lights shut off, drowning the room in darkness.

With an aggravated snort, Domino snapped his fingers, and a soft copper glow burst into existence above his head, illuminating the circle of bunks and most of the bay. Despite having sufficient light, Z and Echo did the same with their magic. Deep blue and dark-gray glows flared above their respective bunks.

Z chuckled softly. "So much for lights out. Please don't tell me that was the amazing part."

Domino pointed at the closed door. "No, I was talking about Major Winters' *smile*. You saw it, right? I didn't think he was capable of making that shape with his mouth. I thought he'd permanently disconnected the muscles there."

Echo sighed wistfully and propped her chin on her hand like she'd fallen in love with a dreamy version of the major. "I wanna see him cry."

"Whoa, whoa." Z lifted her hands but couldn't fight

back another laugh. "Take it easy, okay? Humans can only take so much in a given period of time. If you make them all cry in the first twenty-four hours, what's left?"

The goth searched the upper edge of her dark-gray glow and shrugged. "Making him scream, beg for his life, and call for his mommy."

Domino snorted. "You're so fucked up."

"Uh-huh. Says the pixie who will eat anything and can look like anybody but doesn't know what he wants *Domino* Thornbrook to look like."

He pointed at his sister and grinned. "Touché."

Echo spread her arms and dipped her head as far as she could while lying on her side in bed. She might have been offering an awkward bow, or she might have been stretching.

"I guess we should get some sleep, then," Z commented without moving.

They burst out laughing.

"*Oh five hundred*," Domino grumbled in an impressive impersonation of Major Winters. "He means a.m., right? For what? Magical bootcamp?"

"OIP bootcamp," Z corrected. "We're special, Dom. Don't forget that."

"That's one of the dumbest things I've heard from a human's mouth. A magical Army program with *bootcamp* first. What are they gonna have us do, climb ropes? Do pushups? They realize we can fly and carry thirty times our body weight, right?"

"They don't realize anything. The longer we're here, the more sure I am that the Army is where humans put their morons. They give them weapons to make 'em feel useful."

"Or to keep the troublemakers out of the way." Domino turned over on his stomach, folded his arms on his Army-issue pillow, and laid his head on top of them. "Like us, right?"

"Meh. I think that's still TBD."

"Oipcamp," Echo inserted.

The other pixies forgot about their previous conversation as they shifted on their bunks to look at Echo.

"Uh…" Domino chuckled uncertainly. "If somebody poisoned you and you're going crazy, blink twice."

"Say it one more time," Z added. "I'm not sure what I just heard, so maybe *I* got poisoned."

"Oipcamp," the goth repeated as she looked at her brother and cousin. "Bootcamp for the OIP."

"The fuck?"

"OIP." Echo stared blankly at her brother. "I know we learned to read a *long* time ago, but that's no excuse for forgetting how to sound shit out."

"Oip." He rolled the word around on his tongue, then laughed. "With a stupid name like that, they might as well call us the Flying Pigs."

Z pointed at him and nodded. "So *that's* what they mean by 'when pigs fly.'"

The three pixies' laughter echoed down the halls.

"You gotta be fucking kidding me! Not *one* of you heard the alarm?"

Even Major Winters' shouting the next morning at 4:55 a.m., combined with the aforementioned wakeup alarm blaring through the bay, wasn't enough to pull three pixies from their deep slumber. That made him angrier, so he stormed into the bay and headed for Domino, who was curled up in his Army-issue blankets.

"On your feet, soldier! This is not a drill!"

Domino's mouth popped open, and a snore emerged. The other two pixies didn't stir.

Fuming already, Winters grabbed the edges of Domino's bedsheets and tugged them with both hands. Sheet, blanket, pillow, and pixie toppled over the edge of the bunk and landed heavily on the floor. The major started to step back, but Domino was faster.

Startled out of his sleep by thumping onto the bay floor, the pixie let out a furious shout and rolled onto his hands and knees, then lashed out and swept both of Winters' feet out from under him.

The major hit the floor, and the bay was quiet again.

Then Major Winters groaned and rolled off his tailbone.

That was all it took to wake the other two pixies.

Z growled, "Let me at him. I'll rip his fucking head off!"

Echo used her magical speed and jerked the bedding off her bunk. In seconds, Winters was wrapped in sheets and fighting to get out like a small animal trapped in a burlap sack.

"Who is it?" Z asked as she leapt out of bed. "What is it?"

"Um..." Domino scratched the side of his head, blinked wearily, and yawned. "I think it's Major Winters."

"Ya *think*?" Winters' muffled voice came through the bedsheet Echo had firmly wrapped around him. "I swear by every unholy curse, if y'all don't get this sheet off me right now—"

"Major Winters?" Z asked groggily. "Is that you?"

The major stopped struggling. "I should've put in for a raise before I started this program."

"If it's you," Domino called, cupping both hands around his mouth despite being three feet from the Winters-shaped mummy, "blink twice. Wait. Never mind."

"Just say, 'It's me,'" Z added helpfully.

The major growled, "It's me."

Domino glanced at his sister, then narrowed his eyes at the bedsheet. "Me *who*?"

The mummy didn't offer a reply, but it did start to tremble and emitted a furious huff every few seconds.

Z took a step back. "Yeah, okay. Echo? Maybe you should ease up."

The goth frowned and shook her head.

"Well, it's either our boss or a bomb. You decide."

"Ooh." Domino grinned. "Maybe it's both."

"That's what I was going for, yeah."

That bit of crosstalk was enough of a distraction to loosen Echo's hold on the sheets. Major Winters took advantage of it with a violent swing of his arms and a furious roar. The sheets were ripped out of Echo's hands, and the major flapped around on the floor for a good five seconds before he freed himself.

The second the sheet dropped away from his face, Winters sucked in a breath, tossed the rest of the fabric aside, and climbed to his feet in record time. "In uniform! Beds made! Five minutes!"

He stormed across the bay and disappeared through the door.

The pixies stared at each other, then Domino cleared his throat. "Is it just me, or did it sound like he wanted us to do those things?"

Z shrugged. "Can't hurt to get ready for the day."

Echo glared at the door, then shook a clawed hand in that direction. "Palm of my hand."

"What?"

"I had him in the palm of my hand," she seethed.

"Technically, you had him in a bedsheet, so not really."

Z clapped and sent a *crack* echoing through the bay. "Uniforms and beds. Let's try not to make the major explode next time, okay? I'm not interested in cleaning blood and guts off everything in this room."

Echo snorted. "Speak for yourself."

CHAPTER SIXTEEN

Exactly five minutes later, Major Winters marched back into the bay with a scowl, looking as if he'd never left. Z did notice that the previously pulsing vein at his temple had settled down, however.

Winters glanced at the six bunks the pixies had shoved together to make their sleep circle. While they'd only been given enough bedsheets for one bunk each, the major was satisfied with the condition of those three beds.

He was not, however, satisfied with their Army-issue OCP uniforms. His eyes narrowed when he saw three sets of wings poking out of three sloppy uniforms. Winters' gaze settled on Z, and he twirled a finger. "Turn around."

She grimaced. "Something on my back?"

"I said, turn around, Thornbrook." Winters hadn't anticipated the problem caused by all three of his trainees having the same last name.

All three pixies turned to face their respective bunks.

"Not *all* of you," he snapped. "I'm talking to Blue."

"Z." She shot her new boss a pert look over her shoulder.

"Sure." He took one step forward and leaned closer to peer at the bright blue wings emerging from the jagged slits in the back of her OCP shirt. "What did you do to your uniform?"

"I had to let these out." Z turned to face him since that wasn't as weird as facing her bunks and feeling Winters' scrutinizing gaze on her back. "Don't beat yourself up about it, Major. Your tailors had no idea they'd be making uniforms for pixies with wings."

"That's defacing an Army uniform," Winters growled. "It's grounds for a writeup at the very least."

"It's not your fault," Z replied seriously. "But you might wanna talk to the folks who make these things and add, like, Uniform 2.0 for magicals with wings. Assuming your oip goes the way you want it to—"

"My what?"

"Oipcamp." Domino pointed at his sister. "She came up with it. Catchy, right?"

"No. It's not catchy. It's not even a word. It's *letters*. O. I. P." Winters spread his arms in disbelief. "That's how you will refer to it, understand?"

Domino turned to face his CO and lifted his hands in surrender as if the major were aiming a loaded gun at him instead of a furious scowl that was the definition of the phrase "if looks could kill." "You should've picked a better name. There's always gonna be somebody who turns the acronym into a word, and if you don't like the sound of it…"

Z nodded. "Like those awful parents who name their

kids without thinking about what their initials are gonna be. You know, like 'Stephen Tyler Donaldson.'"

"STD," Domino muttered, raising his eyebrows.

"Or 'Hannah Ophelia Robinson.'"

"HOR."

"'Timothy Nathaniel Tallbeck.'"

"TNT. *Hey.*" Domino's frown gave way to a grin and bright-eyed enthusiasm as he turned to his cousin. "That one's badass."

"Yeah." Z shrugged. "But the poor kid's got a hell of a reputation to live up to. What if he doesn't? Automatic disappointment for everyone when they realize he's not, you know, dy-no-*mite*."

They chuckled. Echo, who hadn't turned around, snorted.

"There are a lot of those," Domino added. "ROD. BAD. FUK."

"That's bad parenting right there."

"All right, that's enough!" Major Winters snapped when his faculties returned to him. The babbling pixies stopped talking, though the smirks on their faces remained.

Scratching the back of his head, Winters stared at his recruits. He couldn't believe he'd let them go on for as long as he had.

Keep it together, Winters. You can't afford to let your brain turn to mush just by talking to these idiots. You have to prove to Command that this program will work, so make it work.

"Well, *boo-fucking-hoo*. You didn't get to pick the name!" Winters barked, startling the pixies.

Their smiles widened, but they didn't look as self-confident as they had.

"Magic or no magic, this is the Army, and y'all are *mine*. Shut your mouths and tell me where you hid the damn things."

Z and Domino exchanged uncertain looks, then Z shook her head. "Not sure what you're talking about, Major."

"The scissors."

Domino chuckled. "I feel like I'm missing something. What scissors?"

"The scissors you morons used to cut up your uniforms!" Winters bellowed. When none of the pixies was forthcoming about the location of said tool, he nodded. "You want to play it that way? Fine. I'll find 'em myself. Step aside."

The major walked forward, intending to tear open the storage drawers beneath all six bunks to find the scissors. Before he'd gone more than four steps, the blue-haired pixie stepped into his path. Winters bristled and leaned away.

"I *know* you heard me," he growled. "Get out of my way. You will not be keeping contraband in here now or ever."

"Sorry, Major." The smile on Z's face was now menacing. "Can't let you do that."

"You don't call the shots, pixie. That's what got you into this mess. I said, *move*."

"I said no." The major's face was reddened, and Z stopped smiling. This was a line she wouldn't let any human cross, boss or not. "You're not going through our things."

"Why not?"

Domino tried to be a buffer between their CO and his

easily inflamed cousin. "You probably don't know this about pixies—"

"I don't know a goddamn thing about y'all."

"But we don't have a whole lotta stuff as a rule," Domino continued, unfazed. "What we do have is *ours*, Major."

Winters turned to the male pixie, his scowl turning his face into a pinched, wrinkled version of itself. "You are in the Army now, bub. Nobody owns shit. Now, step aside, or I'll—"

"Sure. Fine." Domino rolled his eyes. "What you're asking us to do is the same as asking a nice young woman to lift up her skirt so you can make sure everything's where it's supposed to be."

That made Winters pause, and his face reflected his disgust and confusion. He took a step back. "What?"

Domino shrugged. "Just saying."

"It's true," Z added.

The glare she fixed on Major Winters was more disconcerting than the warning stare he'd perfected over the last few decades.

Clenching his jaw, the major decided to back down. The last thing he needed was word getting around that he'd done something heinous like checking under their skirts to the Army's first magical recruits, assuming that what they were telling him was true. "Fine. I expect to have those scissors in my hand before lights out. Right now, get rid of the OCPs you trashed and put on new ones without changing a thing."

Z returned to her mocking self and let out a gasp that was only half in jest. The other half was genuine since her new boss had insinuated something she hadn't expected to hear from a military officer.

"Major Winters," she exclaimed.

He stared at her, then his angry scowl morphed into a worried frown. "What?"

"I'm insulted, and that doesn't happen very often."

Domino shook his head and raised his eyebrows. "At all."

"What are you talking about?" the major asked.

She rolled her eyes. "Talk about a need for sensitivity training."

"Goddammit, Blue!"

"Okay." Z spread her arms and gave him a curt nod. "I don't care what you call me. You obviously can't think of anything cleverer than Blue, and that's fine. We can chalk that up to a lack of human imagination."

The major clenched his fists, and his face reddened as it had when he'd fought to escape from Echo's trap. "First day, Recruit, and you're already pushing it."

"You can't assume *any* of us could go through our daily Army lives without space or breathing room for our wings. I hate to say it, Major, but that's taking things too far. I'm seriously insulted."

Winters' eyebrows did a tense dance on his forehead since he couldn't figure out if she was screwing with him or serious. There was a fifty-fifty chance, and he couldn't run the risk of ruining this entire endeavor before it had begun.

He cleared his throat and dipped his head in as much of a conciliatory gesture as he could manage. "Since we're just getting started, I'll give you one chance to speak your mind. After today, a lot more of you's gonna hurt than your feelings, and I won't pause this program's launch for your complaints. What?"

Z cocked her head and studied the major's surly expression. *He means it. The oip commander isn't as much of a hardass as he wants us to think he is. Good to know.*

"Well, Major..." She clasped her hands behind her back in a barely passable at-ease position. "We're pixies. We have wings. Can we hide 'em? Sure, with a strong illusion spell that takes a lotta energy to maintain. That would make it harder to concentrate on other important stuff. You know, like climbing things, planning strategy, war games, and magical bootcamp."

"Get to the point," Winters growled.

"They're still *there*," she finished. "Can't cut 'em off just because the Army doesn't like wings on their soldiers."

"That would be like cutting someone's arm off," Domino added seriously.

"We can't just fold 'em up and tuck 'em into the back of our shirts, either."

"That's like folding up someone's arm inside their shirt 'cause there's no hole to put it through."

The major looked at them, then gestured at the front of Domino's OCP shirt. "You have arms. And armholes."

Z snickered. "They're called sleeves, Major." He glared at her, but she didn't give him time to react to her smartass comment. "We can't do what we're supposed to do if we can't let our extra appendages air out and flap free. Know what I mean?"

He clenched his eyes shut. "Not an image I needed first thing in the morning."

"They're not *bad*," Domino added in his best rendition of a pleading voice. He jerked a thumb over his shoulder at the copper wings protruding from the slits in his shirt. "We didn't desecrate the uniforms. It was a necessary modification."

Z nodded. "You want us to perform at our best, don't you?"

Winters couldn't stop thinking about the vague warnings Carmine had given him about working with pixies. "That doesn't exactly inspire my confidence."

Z nodded sympathetically. "You'll be a whole lot *less* confident if your first oip guinea pigs screw the project over because they're too physically restricted to do their jobs. Right?"

Domino nodded.

"Fine. Whatever." Major Winters waved angrily. "Keep the damn wing holes, but *that's* not gonna slide."

When he pointed at Echo's back, which was still turned to him, exposing her shimmering black wings, Z and Domino looked at her.

"Whoa. That's harsh, don't you think?" Domino gestured at his sister. "There's nothing wrong with Echo."

Having been addressed for the first time since Winters' order to turn around, Echo spun toward the major and pointed at her chest. Her question was clear. "Who, me?"

"Not her as a person. Or whatever." The major's frown deepened as he tried to figure out the best way to categorize his recruits without further insulting them. "But I can't have a trainee running around with all-black OCPs. I don't care how she got them like that, but wings or no wings, that is not regulation."

The two other pixies eyed Echo as the silent pixie dropped her hand to her side and glared at Winters.

Domino snorted. "Good luck with that."

"Say what?"

"She only wears black."

"Not under *my* command, she doesn't." The major stared at Echo and lowered his head to make himself look more imposing. "Take that off and put on a real uniform."

"Major?" Z raised a hand but didn't wait for him to call on her. "That's a waste of time."

"No, that's the Army. Grab the extra uniform that was given to you, go into the bathroom, and change. I'll wait."

When Echo looked at her brother and cousin for clarification, Domino shrugged.

Z sighed, which the major chose to ignore in lieu of teaching them a quick but necessary lesson in standard operating procedures and uniform regulation. "We gotta do what he says now, Echo."

"For as long as you are on this base and under my command," Winters added, "you're damn right you do. Now move it, Recruit. That's an order."

With a grudging sigh, Echo knelt in front of the drawer beneath her bunk and took out the second uniform she'd been given. She didn't bother to close the drawer before stalking across the bay without a glance at anyone. The bay's metal door squealed open and thunked shut.

Then it was just Major Winters and the two pixies who could talk to him. That wasn't ideal, but he would work with what he had.

After another minute of awkward silence, Domino

blew a raspberry, sounding more like a horse than a pixie. Or a soldier. "It's not gonna matter—"

"No talking," Winters snapped. "From either of you."

"I'm just sayin'," Domino continued under his breath.

Z shot her cousin a sidelong glance that would look like a warning from the outside. Both of them were fighting not to laugh about what they knew would happen when Echo reentered the bay.

Another minute passed. Major Winters growled, "I haven't forgotten about the contraband. Where are the goddamn scissors?"

The pixies stared at him like they'd gone catatonic.

"That wasn't a rhetorical question, Recruits."

Z grimaced and gazed all over the bay. "You said no talking, Major."

"When I'm questioning you directly, give me a goddamn answer!"

"Right, right. Okay." She lifted both hands in concession. "Jeez. I had no idea the rules were this complicated."

"We weren't lying," Domino added. "Plus, we couldn't even *find* scissors."

"Yeah, Corporal Packard wasn't all that helpful. How's he doing, by the way? He looked out of it when he left us here."

"We were worried."

"Corporal Packard's none of your business." The major inhaled and closed his eyes. *These numbskulls are more literal than the dictionary.* "If you didn't take scissors to the uniforms, what *did* you use?"

Z chuckled. "Magic."

He paused, then leaned toward her and murmured blankly, "What?"

"Magic. Spells." She wiggled her fingers. "*Hoodoo*. Right? Isn't that what you humans call it?"

Their CO looked like his ability to think was going to follow the same path as Corporal Packard's. Domino added, "The thing that makes us magicals from Oriceran, Major. *Magic*. Come on. Don't tell us you've forgotten about it?"

"Not a *small* detail." Z cracked a smile even though she was concerned for him. "Especially when you created a whole program based on—"

"*Then why would y'all ask Corporal Packard for scissors?*"

His tone made the pixies consider their answer. Dominic shrugged. "Seemed like the best way to fit in."

"Lord help me." The major pinched the bridge of his nose and took slow, deep breaths with his eyes closed.

"We thought that's what you wanted." Z pursed her lips. "As much as three magicals in a special Army program can fit in."

"Did I give you permission to speak freely?" Winters snapped. "Zip it."

He thought he'd finally gotten through to them when both pixies shut their mouths and stared blankly ahead. Then Domino lifted a hand to his face and mimed pulling a zipper across his lips.

Z tried to hold it together, but her cousin let out a choked honk, and she lost it.

Shaking his head, Winters clasped his hands behind his back and spun to pace across the bay. *They're trying their damnedest to get under my skin. That's all this is. Just act like you don't give a shit, and they'll straighten out.*

It made sense when dealing with moody teenagers and juvenile delinquents. But with pixies who clearly don't care about the rules and who had only agreed to join his program because it was the best of two terrible options, Winters wasn't sure it was going to work.

He couldn't threaten them with arrest and confinement since Carmine Ratchetter was gone, so there was no one on site who was remotely qualified to round up three pixies and force them back into the magic-containment room. He couldn't threaten them with a dishonorable discharge since that was likely what they were hoping for, and how would a writeup motivate these pissants into taking this seriously?

I gotta find out what they do take seriously and use it as a carrot or a stick. Would've been nice if the gnome had told me what that was before he up and disappeared.

He tuned out Z's and Domino's laughter as he paced back across the bay. The metallic clang of the door being jerked open surprised them all, and all three turned to the open door. Echo stalked back in with the black-dyed OCP uniform neatly folded in her arms.

Major Winters clenched his fists, and it occurred to him that forcing himself not to blow up wasn't doing his high blood pressure any favors. "What is that?"

Without looking at him, Echo shrugged and stalked toward her bunk. She dumped the first uniform into the open drawer.

The major pointed at her and tried to ignore the trembling in his arm. "What do you think you're doing? I told you black OCPs are against regulations."

"And *we* told you it was a waste of time," Domino muttered in a singsong voice as he swept his gaze around the room. "She only wears black."

"She was in there for five goddamn minutes with a standard-reg set. Look at this…this… Even the *boots!*"

Echo turned to face him without expression and spread her arms.

"Uh-uh." Winters shook his head. "Get your ass back out there and put on a uniform that isn't a joke!"

His shout echoed around the bay.

Z cleared her throat. "Major?"

He whirled toward her and bellowed, *"What?"*

She was unfazed by his outburst. "Corporal Packard only gave us two uniforms each."

"He only…" Winters blinked and spun toward the door. "We're way behind schedule, so keep up."

When he didn't say anything else, the Thornbrook pixies shared a knowing look.

Domino rubbed his hands together and grinned. "First day on the job, kids. Better bring Mommy and Daddy a good report, huh?"

He took off after Major Winters, and his sister and cousin followed closely.

Z eyed Echo as they crossed the room. "Not gonna lie. That looks badass on you."

Echo stared straight ahead but let the corners of her mouth curl up in a satisfied smile.

CHAPTER SEVENTEEN

Z and her cousins didn't know that being escorted to the mess hall for morning chow by their major wasn't part of regular Army bootcamp. Nor were they aware that their initial training schedule had been tweaked with a heavy dose of creative license on Major Winters' part so it contained the bare bones of Basic Training but none of the fun.

Not for the COs and the small team of Special Forces soldiers who'd been selected to take part in the OIP with three obnoxious pixies.

That elite team was sitting in the facility's mess hall with their breakfast trays.

Major Winters looked like he'd swallowed a live cockroach as he led the pixies across the mess hall, scowling in disgust and discomfort. The tables were on the other side of the medium-sized room, so Z and her cousins had plenty of time to scrutinize the dozen soldiers quietly shoveling down their morning chow.

It was also plenty of time for the soldiers to take a good long look at the three newcomers. The pixies could have passed for normal humans if it hadn't been for their wings. Also, one of them had been allowed to show up for her first day of training in an all-black uniform.

They'd crossed half the room before Domino couldn't keep his mouth shut any longer. "Hey, Z," he started, his voice rising enough for everyone to hear. "Aren't those the punks with guns we knocked to the ground a few days ago?"

Z smirked and played along. "Hmm. We've dropped a lotta punks, man. You're gonna have to be a little more specific."

"In the woods. You know, when they started shooting at us and couldn't hit anything but a rotting log."

"Oh, *those* punks." Z stared at the soldiers, who had stopped eating their breakfast. She narrowed her eyes and let out a noncommittal hum as she scrutinized their faces. "You know what? I think you're right. It's just hard to recognize 'em without all that gear and the looks of terror."

Echo paused at the second table and stared at the soldier sitting at the end. He stared back at her with his fork raised halfway to his mouth, and when he realized the creepy-looking chick with black hair and an all-black Army uniform wasn't going to back down, he dropped his fork on his plate and leaned toward her. "What the fuck are *you* looking at, Tinkerbell?"

Domino stopped in his tracks and spun to glare at the soldier. "What did you just call her?"

"That's what you are, isn't it?" The soldier didn't look

away from Echo, though his eyes did narrow when she leaned toward him and spread her arms to egg him on.

"Seriously?" Domino stomped toward his sister. "That's the best you could come up with? Tinkerbell?"

A wry chuckle escaped him through a smile that made him look insane. He slapped his sister's arm with the back of a hand and nodded. "You hear that? Dumb soldier thinks making up words makes him scary."

The soldier laughed, then turned to the others at his table, who were watching the strange interaction. "Is this asshole for real?"

"Listen, *pal*." That got the soldier's attention, and he spun back to Domino with a glare. "If you're gonna insult a pixie, try using your brain for some *real* words."

"I'd watch your fucking mouth, Peter Pan," the soldier growled.

Echo whispered in Domino's ear. He snickered. "She says you might wanna look for your intelligence in the woods from the other night 'cause she's the one who slapped it out of you."

"Fuck this shit!" The soldier rose to his full six-foot-three to tower over the pixies. "Say that again."

Although he was a foot and a half taller than her, Echo didn't flinch. She took a step toward the seething soldier, lifted her chin, and waved him toward her with both hands.

The soldier's abrupt movement and the screech of his chair on the tile floor caught Major Winters' attention. He surveyed the heated situation, which was growing hotter by the second, and his decades of being an officer kicked in.

"Lindon!" he barked. "Put your ass back in that seat and cut the bullshit!"

Everyone in the room froze, then Lindon lowered himself back into his seat, keeping his glare on Domino.

"*That's* right," the pixie muttered. "Cut the bullshit like a good little doggie."

"Front and center, Recruits," Winters bellowed. "*Now!*"

Echo stayed where she was, staring at the soldier, who'd returned his attention to finishing his morning chow. Domino stepped back and scanned the room.

He turned to the major with a confused frown. "I don't get it. Those are two different things."

It took all of Winters' remaining willpower not to storm across the mess hall and slap the male pixie. "It's not your job to get it, Recruit. It's your job to follow orders."

"Well, sure, but are they always gonna be this confusing?"

The dozen soldiers who'd been enjoying their breakfast until the three pixies had entered the room all stared at Domino. They couldn't fathom how anyone who'd been brought into a program like Major Winters' OIP, magical or not, had the balls to speak to his commanding officer like that.

Winters gaped, his brain seconds from frying after the morning he'd had with these recruits. He flinched and leaned away when Z was suddenly at his side.

She pointed at the middle of the room between the four long tables and murmured, "The center of the room's over there. The front? Is that back by the door or somewhere else?"

His eyes widened when he realized how literal his recruits were. Then his faculties returned.

"It means get your asses over here," he called to Domino and Echo. "Right now."

"*Oh.*" Z folded her arms and nodded. "That's a funny way of saying it, but hey. If a secret Army code makes you feel special, go for it, right? Might be helpful to have a dictionary for that."

He growled, "Back the hell up, Recruit."

Feigning surprise, Z lifted both hands and did so.

Her cousins grudgingly pulled themselves away from what might have turned into another pixie-on-Special-Forces showdown. They approached Z and the red-faced, tight-jawed Major Winters.

He glared at each of his new recruits in turn. "This is Day One. Don't make me regret giving y'all a shot at this. If you fuck this up, I *will* shut down this program. Then it won't matter if you want to go back home. That's where y'all are headed if this doesn't work out. Got it?"

"You talk a good game, Major." Z winked. "But you took the only three pixies left behind because that's all you had. You *need* us."

The major narrowed his eyes, and for the first time since circumstances had thrust them together, Z didn't see an ounce of uncertainty in the man's gaze.

"Wanna bet?" he replied flatly. "Y'all aren't the only magicals out there making too much trouble to be left alone. The second this thing goes south, your contracts are over. Then there's nothing standing between you and Oriceran or me and a squad of magicals that isn't a pain in my ass. You want to know what *I* think?"

Wrinkling his nose, Domino shrugged. "Not really."

"I think *you* need *me*." Winters raised his eyebrows and glanced at each pixie's face. "Now, load up a tray, take a seat, play nice, and eat your chow. You got ten minutes."

He surprised all of them by stalking back across the mess hall toward the door. He didn't say another word to the three pixies or the dozen Special Forces troops.

The metal door screeched open, then banged shut. The room fell into a tense, anticipatory silence.

Z grabbed a tray and a plate to start loading on breakfast. Domino and Echo followed suit. They could feel the spiteful gazes of a dozen soldiers on their backs.

As she spooned on a sloppy helping of what could have been oatmeal, Z dipped her head and smirked. "You heard him, guys. The major wants us to play nice."

Domino snickered as he grabbed an enormous helping of bacon with a pair of tongs.

"What do you think?" Z continued, shooting her cousins a sidelong glance.

"Sounds good to me," Domino murmured.

Echo didn't have to look at what she was doing. She stabbed her fork into a platter of sliced ham, skewering four slices and rattling all the dishes on the table. The corners of her mouth quirked a macabre smile of which only a goth pixie was capable. "Okay, then."

Z absently grabbed the pitcher of orange juice and filled a glass to the brim. "Let's kick off Day One."

The Thornbrooks had been making trouble and handling the resulting sticky situations as a team for so long that they didn't have to say more than that. Calinda and her gang had dubbed them "the triplets" because of their uncanny ability to carry out plans without a word.

The rogue pixies had suspected the three could read each other's minds. That wasn't the case, but it was close.

CHAPTER EIGHTEEN

After they'd loaded their trays with more food than any soldier could have stomached, Z and her cousins headed across the mess hall toward the long tables. There were a few soldiers sitting at each, all of whom continued eating in wary silence as they glared at the newcomers.

Z knew which table she would pick before she headed that way. When she reached it, she broke away from her cousins and slid into a chair opposite one of the soldiers whose face she'd recognized the second she'd stepped into the room. He didn't stop staring at her, even when she drained half her glass of orange juice in one gulp. Setting it gently on the table, she grabbed her fork and met his gaze with a grin. "Hey, there."

Domino and Echo picked separate tables. After he'd plopped into an open seat in front of three soldiers who hadn't said or done anything to piss off the pixies, he dug into his food, ignoring their stares.

Echo went back to the table where Lindon and three other soldiers were trying to finish their meals. Instead of sitting in one of the open chairs at the table, she grabbed one from another table, dragged it noisily across the floor, and set it at the head of the table. Once settled, she spooned food into her mouth without looking at it since she was sweeping her flat, emotionless gaze from one soldier's face to the next.

The mess hall's previous silence was punctured by the sounds of three pixies enthusiastically eating while the dozen soldiers bristled.

For the first few minutes, it seemed as if the elite team and the three magicals might get through the rest of the meal without further altercations.

That wasn't the plan.

Halfway through her meal, Z downed the second half of her orange juice and slammed the glass on the table. The three soldiers near her looked up from their plates or jerked their silverware to the side, expecting another bout of magical mayhem that might have rivaled the shitshow that had been their first OIP mission in the woods.

Z only cared about one soldier, which was why she'd taken the empty seat across from him. She didn't have to study his expression to guess what was going through his head.

He remembers me too. That makes this even better.

She feigned recognition and widened her smile. "*Hey!* You look really familiar."

The soldier's upper lip twitched, and he shot a glance at the other members of his team at the table. He muttered, "No shit."

"Yeah, *now* it's coming back." Z wagged a finger at him

and kept a straight face so she could play this out a little longer. "Sorry. Took me a bit to put it together."

She moved the food around on the plate with her fork, then flicked her gaze back at him. "I almost didn't recognize you when you weren't pissing your pants and screaming like a little girl."

Under different circumstances, the rest of the team would've found her trash-talk hilarious, especially coming from a new addition to their unit. However, these soldiers had recently had that brief and painful encounter with Oriceran magicals, which hadn't turned out well for them.

Those same Oriceran magicals were sitting in their mess hall, sharing their tables, eating their food, ignoring their chain of command, and damaging standard Army Operational Camouflage Pattern uniforms so everyone here could get a good look at their wings.

Z saw the soldier remembered the moment in the woods when a glowing blue two-inch-tall woman with blue hair had ripped his firearm out of his hands and used it to club him in the head.

He wanted to leap across the table and throttle the magical who was pretending to be like him and the rest of the team in both size and service in the Army. Instead, knowing he and the rest of his team would have to deal with these winged freaks for the duration of the program, he scooped up the last forkful of his scrambled eggs and muttered, "You won't make it past the first week."

"Ooh." Z shimmied her shoulders in excitement and smiled wider. "Challenge accepted. Normally, I'm not the one starting bets, but I'm feeling pretty lucky today. So, wanna bet on that?"

The soldier shot his buddies another look that asked if they were hearing all this, then crammed the last bite of eggs into his mouth and growled, "Fuck off."

Domino had the same luck at his table with the three soldiers with whom he'd chosen to share his meal. He managed to maintain a wide grin through every bite, cramming his mouth with impressive speed and efficiency. When he judged the tension at his table had reached a sufficient level, he turned his crumb-covered grin on the soldiers trying to ignore him. "You know what I can't get off my mind?"

The soldier at the opposite end of the table downed the rest of his coffee. "No one gives a shit."

"Your little friend over there made up a bunch of words earlier," Domino continued, completely unphased by the reaction. "Tinkerbell. Peter Pan. Well, Peter is a name, but the rest of it? I can't figure it out. Is it an actual pan? Who named it, and why did they name it *Peter*?"

The soldiers at the table stiffened in irritation, befuddled as to why their commanding officer had officially brought in a pixie, especially one who blabbed on about a character from a fairytale like he had no idea who it was.

They didn't say anything because they were aware of the possibility of violence. Lashing out the way they wanted to would make the team no better than a ragged platoon of green recruits in Basic Training.

Unfortunately for them, pixies were relentless. The only time their patience lasted longer than their generally short fuse was when they were working toward a goal they intended to fulfill. It was even better when that goal was meaningless and detrimental to everyone else.

Domino was no exception.

"It's a hell of a brain-buster, that's for sure." He crammed half a piece of toast into his mouth, spraying buttered crumbs all over the table and on several of the soldiers' plates as he kept talking. "I wasn't kidding about him getting his head checked. You should probably talk to him about that. He'll listen to his brothers with arms. That's what you guys call each other, right? Or is it, like, a little more…private?"

With raised eyebrows and a big smile, he scanned every face at the table as if they were all in on a private joke and he was the one bringing it up.

"Nah, you know what? Don't tell me. I don't need to know what you guys get up to when you're alone together with doors closed. I won't ask, and you won't tell, huh?"

Domino crammed the other half of his messy toast into his mouth while barking a laugh. Crumbs spewed from his mouth to pepper the soldiers' uniforms. Two of the soldiers lurched away from the table with grunts of disgust.

Domino pretended not to notice as he rambled on. "Seriously," he added through another spray of crumbs. "I think you guys should get looked at for concussions. Internal bleeding. Maybe brain-swelling. What do they call that? Cerebral enema? Whatever it is. That night in the woods was rough, am I right? I mean, for *you* guys. A dozen grown dudes against a dozen pixies, and none of you lasted more than, what, three minutes? That's being too generous. We really spanked your asses out there."

He paused, waiting for a reaction, the use of incorrect phrases, or a general dumb and clueless act. The only thing he wasn't faking was how thoroughly he was enjoying himself.

Just when he thought he would have to start another infuriating round while the soldiers angrily swiped his toast crumbs off their uniforms and pushed their contaminated plates away, one of them leaned forward and lowered his voice to a deep, warning growl. "You and all those freaks might've gotten the drop on us the other night, but you're not in the woods anymore, Tinkerbell."

"Oh, come *on*!" Domino slapped a hand on the table. "You're gonna use the nonsense word your buddy made up?"

The soldier ignored his comment and narrowed his eyes. "This is the *Army*, asshole, and in case you hadn't noticed, there are still a dozen of us but only three of *you* now."

Domino closed his mouth to finish chewing his toast, which allowed him to smirk. He delayed his response to let the puffed-up human think he'd gotten through, but when that soldier leaned back and started to finish his breakfast, Domino seized the opportunity. "You know what, champ?"

The soldier slammed his fork back onto his plate and gave the pixie a murderous glare. His colleagues shifted in their seats, clenching their jaws and fists. They were clearly fighting their inherent, or maybe Army-induced, instincts to engage and neutralize the threat in front of them.

Domino ignored them. He picked up his glass of milk and casually raised it to his lips. "I gotta admit I'm impressed. That's a good, strong scare statement without delivering a real threat. It could use a little work, though. Some imagination. You know, get creative with it. Tell me you're gonna tear my wings off with a pair of pliers or punch out my teeth to wear as a necklace or something. Really spice it up."

The soldier was baffled. He was out of moves.

Domino closed his eyes and drained the glass of milk in one breath, then smacked his lips and let out a contented sigh. "Don't worry. I won't hold it against you. You're obviously a beginner at this kinda thing. If you want any tips on how to be *really* scary, I'll be happy to help."

Another soldier at the end of the table snorted and shook his head. "Little shit's out of his fucking mind."

"Aw." The grin Domino flashed him was so wide it made his nose wrinkle. He looked like a wild animal baring its teeth. "That's so cute."

He put a cherry on top of the screwing-with-elite-soldiers sundae by using magic to emphasize his point—and hopefully prod these humans into acting on the rage they were trying *so* hard to keep at bay.

The human soldiers each saw something different. One would have sworn the magical's brown eyes glowed red, which reminded him of the demonic creatures he thought he believed in.

Another saw razor-sharp teeth behind the pixie's mad grin, complete with a set of inch-long fangs winking in the mess hall's overhead light. The third froze in horror when Domino's face morphed into the features of a man he'd spent the last decade and a half trying to forget. Until that moment, he'd thought he'd succeeded.

The psychic manipulation only lasted two seconds. When it was over, they stared at him, speechless and stunned by what they'd seen. Even more fun was the knowledge that when they got together to talk about what had happened, none of them would have seen the same thing. Then they'd start questioning their sanity, which was what the pixie was counting on.

It would make them easier to deal with in the coming months of training.

It's like they just slapped a few ideas together and called it a plan, he thought. *This is ridiculous.*

Then there was Echo.

CHAPTER NINETEEN

While all this was happening at Z's and Domino's tables, the goth pixie had dedicated her focus to one simple yet effective method. She didn't utter a word, but she didn't have to.

After she'd met the wary gaze of every soldier at her table, she turned her attention to Lindon. The thick slices of ham on her plate were large enough that all she had to do was prop an elbow on the table, hold her fork in front of her mouth, and occasionally bite off another chunk.

She did that with ferocity, although her movements were concise and calm.

The ham was just part of the display. Leaning over the end of the table, Echo kept her dark narrow-eyed gaze on Lindon's face. For the first several minutes, the tension at the table thickened as the other soldiers looked up from their plates to gauge the goth's unwavering intensity and Lindon's decision to focus on his breakfast. He didn't look at any other members of his team, and he didn't spare Echo a second glance.

He didn't know she could sit there all day and had done so on multiple occasions when a stare-down was called for by pixie justice. The longer Echo stared at the soldier she'd targeted, the more sensitive Lindon became. He started to feel the pixie's gaze on him like an itch that wouldn't go away. It reminded him of walking through a spiderweb, but he'd be damned if he would swipe at his face to get rid of the feeling.

The intensity of the sensation grew, and so did his irritation. He was barely aware of the tense conversations elsewhere in the room—Z's taunts and Domino's senseless chatter—but the words buzzed through his mind.

The spiderweb feeling on his face took on weight and solidity as Lindon's irritation flared into cold, hard rage.

He lasted another four minutes before he couldn't take it anymore and stopped thinking. Slamming his fork on his tray, he glared at the goth. She didn't bat an eye. "You still got a problem?"

Echo didn't move.

The other humans at the table exchanged dubious glances. The one sitting closest to Lindon shook his head to remind the guy that taking it further would get the team smoked to hell and back because they knew better.

Lindon didn't notice. "Go ahead." He jerked his chin toward Echo, then leaned back in his chair and spread his arms. "Fucking say it."

She tilted her head but said nothing. It was clear to everyone else at the table that the guy was about to lose his shit, and there was nothing they could do to stop it. That didn't stop them from trying.

"Hey, man," the soldier beside him muttered, putting a steadying hand on Lindon's shoulder. "Just let it go."

"No, fuck that. I wanna know what this freak thinks is so goddamn interesting about my face."

"Lindon," another soldier murmured. "It's just part of the job. Fucking cool it, huh?"

"You first, Bixby." Lindon pointed at the guy sitting across from him, then turned his gaze on Bixby. A silent message passed between them, similar to those shared by Z and her cousins after having spent so much time together in various situations. For a full ten seconds, Lindon glared at the soldier who was trying to help, then remembered who and what he was and got hold of his emotions. "Fuck it."

He relaxed and went back to eating. It looked like the pressure had been diffused by his buddies.

That wasn't acceptable to Echo Thornbrook.

Without breaking her stare or moving a muscle on her expressionless face, she held another slice of ham beside her mouth and flicked her index finger at Lindon.

A glob of cold, gelatinous oatmeal flew off Bixby's plate and hit Lindon in the center of his forehead.

"You fairy piece of shit!" Lindon lurched up from his chair, overturning his coffee cup and rattling the trays and dishes on the table.

"Whoa, whoa!" The other soldiers rose and tried to hold him back, but he jerked his arms out of their hands and stormed around the table too quickly for them to catch him.

When he reached the end of the table and loomed over

Echo, he was red in the face and breathing heavily. "What's wrong? No more table between us. Whatcha gonna do?"

"Lindon, come on," someone else called. "Leave it."

"Aw, shit. Give it to her, Lindon."

"Somebody's gotta teach those morons a lesson."

"Not such a badass without all your other freaky little friends, huh?"

Echo remained calm while the mess hall filled with shouts from the rest of the Army unit. The soldiers were split between encouraging Lindon to turn their first official meeting with the new OIP pixies into a violent altercation and backing down so they didn't all get their asses handed to them when their program commander found out.

The soldiers sitting at the other three tables seemed to have forgotten about Z and Domino.

"You got a serious problem, and I'm done letting it slide," Lindon goaded as he towered over the goth. "If you wanna hit me for real, bitch, fucking hit me. Let's go!"

The man's rage had taken over. If Echo hadn't been so focused on playing out the plan, she would have laughed in the guy's face. Instead, she lowered her fork and the ham to her plate and gazed up at the furious soldier.

His fury stoked by her calm gaze, Lindon tensed his arm, either to swing a fist into the black-haired pixie's face or grab her by the collar of her far-from-standard OCP shirt and haul her to her feet. He hadn't decided which.

Before he moved, Echo reverted to pixie size and launched her tray into the soldier's face.

All hell broke loose.

The tray clattered to the floor. Lindon roared in disgust and rage. The other soldiers at the table leapt up to join the second fight between the Special Forces unit and the pixies.

It was exactly what Z and Domino had been trying to instigate, though Echo was usually the one to get the party started.

The soldiers at Domino's table jumped to their feet to see what had happened at Lindon's table. It looked like the stone-faced pixie chick had vanished into thin air.

"Man, your buddy swings like a girl," Domino taunted. "The human kind."

The soldiers started to run to the other table to join the four men swatting at the dark-gray light flitting through the air, but they stopped when Domino let out a lunatic cackle and sprang onto the table, knocking trays and plates and silverware to the floor. "Hold on, guys. You really think you're getting outta this that easy?"

When they turned to see an insane-looking pixie crouching on the table, Domino pointed at the globs of food on the floor. Several flashed a bright pulse of copper light and flew at the soldiers.

Shouting, cursing, and wiping scrambled egg and congealed oatmeal from their eyes, the men forgot about Lindon's struggle and turned their ire on the pixie at their table.

Giggling, Domino pointed at them. "What a look!"

While the commotion echoed around the mess hall, the blue-glowing pixie recognized this as the perfect opportunity to get sneakier. She shrank to her natural size and flitted toward the serving tables. Snickering, she hovered behind the pot holding the now-cold oatmeal and waited for the thickheaded humans to notice that something else wasn't quite right.

Copper and gray light zipped across the temporary mess hall, along with strips of bacon, globs of scrambled egg, slices of ham, and silverware. Even over the furious shouts, growls, and grunts from half a dozen seasoned soldiers, it was impossible to miss the wild cackling of the pixie troupe.

When Maass, the soldier Z had been intent on throwing off the deep end, turned back to see what the third pixie was up to, he looked around wildly because she wasn't at the table anymore.

It took him another second to notice that the extra helpings of morning chow were floating above the serving tables. Then he saw the blue glow behind the oatmeal pot. All the color drained from his face.

A tiny, high-pitched, but recognizable voice called with surprising volume from behind that pot, "You won't make it past the next five minutes!"

"Oh, shit!" He tried to dive under the table to keep from being splattered by the floating food, but before he got his body to obey his brain's commands, two streaks of glowing light, one copper and the other dark gray, shot past his right shoulder. A soldier crashed into Maass' bicep in his desperate pursuit of the pixies, and they hit the table.

Wood splintered, metal legs squealed, and the table buckled in the center. Then the oatmeal pot's contents rose and splattered both of them.

Z zipped up to the ceiling, towing the floating bits of food after her to continue the food fight.

The odds were heavily skewed in the team's favor. That didn't mean squat when they were up against any number of pixies, but it meant even less against the three who had been crazy and reckless enough to take the Army's deal.

That quickly became apparent to the team. To Z's surprise and delight, Lindon was the first to abandon the fight. The soldier fled across the mess hall, clutching at his fellow soldiers' sleeves and tugging them along with him. Then he abandoned attempting to tell them it was time to give up and retreat. The others had come to the same conclusion, however, and a dozen grown men and women in uniform scrambled past the overturned tables and chairs, slipping on globs of chow scattered across the floor.

Food flew across the room after them. Several were stopped in their tracks by invisible slaps or sharp, painful tugs on their hair. Their urgent shouts to get the hell out of there echoed behind them, and the metal door continuously crashed against the wall as the soldiers threw it open one by one and disappeared into the hall.

In seconds, the only sound in the mess hall was high-pitched laughter.

Domino flew in loops, copper light trailing behind him. Z darted toward the door as it swung shut for the final time, peeking at the last of the soldiers stumbling and staggering and slipping down the hall.

"Aw, come on, guys," she called after them. "What's wrong? We were playing nice!"

Echo cackled for a long time, sinking a few inches before her black wings lifted her. When she regained control of herself, her laughter cut off abruptly, and her face returned to its blank mask. "Fucking punks."

"Hey, guys," Domino called as he landed on an overturned table with a giant glob of scrambled egg in one hand. He bit into it, chucked the rest at the closest wall, and chewed. "I think I figured out why it's called a mess hall."

CHAPTER TWENTY

That set the precedent for the rest of the pixies' training.

When Major Winters heard the soldiers' retreat, he left the closet he used as a break room to investigate. After he determined the details, he was unimpressed with everyone's behavior, humans and magicals alike.

He had a much bigger problem than a dozen men deserting their breakfast. Winters caught up with the elite team and gave them a piece of his mind.

"Major, they're insane," Bixby protested after he'd stated his points.

"Fuck insane," Maass added. "They're psychotic."

"You weren't there." Brakeman pulled strings of coagulated cheese out of his hair. "You didn't see what those freaks can do."

"They laughed the whole time."

"Worst fucking day of my whole career. Fucking fairies."

The major frowned as the team went on. When they were done, he gazed at the unit, most of whom were still wearing chow, and took a deep breath. When the soldiers realized what was happening, they looked more terrified than they had when they were getting their asses kicked by a total of six inches of pixie.

"I'm sorry, men," Winters began. "That must've been difficult."

The soldiers shuffled, but nobody dared speak.

"I guess I should send y'all down to the medical center for an evaluation." the major continued. "Give y'all a break to get your heads screwed on straight again. Take a breather.

"While you're down there, I'll have the catering company stop by with a fruit basket and fuzzy robes and slippers. Y'all can stand around holding hands and singing *Kumbaya* while you let your fragile hearts heal from the first day of this program. *Sound good?*"

By this time, the team was standing at attention while their commanding officer screamed in their faces, which was an automatic response.

"No? Nobody likes the sound of that? Well, shit. Now I don't know *what* to do since I thought I had one of the best Special Forces teams in the brigade on this assignment. I only see a bunch of whiny babies who can't handle a few loose screws over chow!"

There weren't many other officers or soldiers in this facility, for good reason. Major Winters had petitioned for a private setting to train his magical recruits so they would not be ogled by the entire detachment at the base during the process. Thus, there was no one else there to see the elite team get chewed out by the major.

That didn't stop them from staring straight ahead, arms

held stiffly at their sides as they bore the verbal consequences of starting a fight with three pixies. And losing.

Major Winters looked them over one more time and grunted. "Go clean yourselves up. I better see every one of you in the PT bay at oh eight hundred, or so help me…"

No one stuck around in case the major finished that sentence. The unit knew he trailed off in the middle of unvoiced threats, and it was *their* job to hop to and do what he'd commanded.

Winters watched them march down the hall, swift and silent and covered in food. When the last soldier disappeared around the corner, he sucked his teeth and closed his eyes.

Figured if I wasn't there for chow, those magical dimwits would act more grateful to be here. Turns out it's not just me. They're dicks to everyone.

With a sigh, he slowly walked toward the mess hall, trying to figure out how he could get the pixies in line.

How did you get somebody to shape up when they didn't give a shit about anything or anyone but themselves?

I couldn't even catch one of 'em to keep in holding until the others clean up their act, let alone all of 'em. I swear, those little shits're likely to run toward a bomb instead of away from it.

He stopped in the middle of the hallway, grateful that he was alone. No one could see him struggling to solve a major piece of the puzzle he hadn't considered before he got his first magical OIP recruits.

There was no one to see the contemplative smile on his lips when Major Winters realized he did have *one* bit of leverage over the pixie trio. It was the only thing they'd revealed about themselves so far, and it had taken him this long to understand what a valuable bargaining chip it was.

"They *do* care about something," he muttered. He laughed darkly as he strode toward the mess hall.

Shoved it right under my nose, and I was too caught up in their words to pay attention, he mused.

He was paying attention now.

When he reached the door to the mess hall, he paused, then grabbed the door and threw it open. Then he walked inside like he knew exactly what to expect and didn't bother to look around the room before bellowing, "Bet you are proud of yourselves, aren't you?"

Winters' boot crunched on a crisp strip of bacon, and he paused to examine the sole. Then he clasped his hands behind his back and scanned the room. "Had a good time chasing out the team that's here to help y'all do your jobs. Hell of a way to kick things off if you ask me."

"We didn't ask you," Z muttered in a normal human tone.

Winters saw her sitting backward on one of the chairs, nibbling on half a piece of toast.

He raised an eyebrow and shrugged. "Still."

With a rattle and a thump, a five-foot pixie with copper wings blinked into existence on the edge of one of the tables. He swung his legs as he crunched into a bruised apple that looked like it had spent the last half-hour being used as a tennis ball. "Well, this is nice. Major Winters is in a cheery mood."

Echo snickered. The sound made Winters pause before he looked straight. The goth was hovering a foot below the ceiling, her chin resting on her folded arms and her legs spread out behind her like she was face-down on a mattress instead of floating in a military mess.

He wanted to throw something at her to get her on the floor. The major chose not to, just returned his gaze to Z and Domino.

"What happened, Major?" Z called. "Get a call that they changed their minds, and you gotta scrap the oip?" Her cousins snorted, and Z's smile widened. Then she popped the rest of the toast into her mouth and chewed.

"No, we're still on," Winters replied, surprising himself with how confident and self-assured he sounded. After the last twenty-four hours, he'd wondered if he'd ever sound like this again. "Y'all can chalk up my good mood to a change in perspective."

"Perspective, huh?" Domino glanced at his sister, who was still floating just below the ceiling. "Like, from somewhere up there?"

Winters clicked his tongue and took a deep breath.

"I have to be honest. First time I walked into that holding cell and saw that only three of y'all had decided to stick around and give this program a try, I was disappointed. What good is an entire program designed for magicals if I only have three to test the damn thing? Almost lost my confidence that OIP had a shot at success. What could three tiny people *do*?"

Domino snorted and took another bite of his apple. Echo sighed, rolled over, and folded her arms behind her head. Z raised an eyebrow and swallowed her mouthful of toast.

That one's going to be tough to crack, Winters thought as

he stepped away from a slimy-looking puddle of unidentifiable chow. *Not as tough as she thinks, though.*

He spread his arms and dropped his gaze to the food-smeared floor, pleased with himself for the performance he was giving.

"But I've been doing this for a long time. The Army, not OIP. I've learned to admit when I'm wrong since that's the first step toward getting anyone under your command to see you as a regular human being like them."

"We're not regular human beings," Z muttered.

"Nah." The major shook his head, "But I'm willin' to bet you are special among your own kind. Don't get me wrong. That shitshow out in the woods? That had me wondering what I'd gotten myself into, and things got screwier from there.

"Twelve on twelve isn't a challenge, even when half are Special Forces and the other half are only two inches tall. However, the same team gettin' their asses handed to 'em by *three* of you? In my book, that's special."

"Major. *Stop!*" Domino flapped a hand at the major and batted his eyes faux bashfully. "You're making me blush."

"So what?" Z added before her cousin could commandeer this unexpected turn of events. "You came in here to congratulate us? This was a piece of cake, and I'm not sure your *elite team* has what it takes to train us in anything other than how to turn tail and run away screaming." Echo hissed a laugh.

Winters kept his cool. He still had his leverage. "No. Y'all haven't done a thing yet to deserve praise, but I figured it might be a morale boost to hear a few words from your CO that aren't about how much you're fucking up. I might even go so far as to say I was impressed."

Z snorted and drawled, "Well, whoopee for us."

The major wiped the small but visible smile off his face and let his scowl return. "But that doesn't change what this is or what we're doing. You are Army pixies now, and the three of you are gonna shape up and start doing as you're told. First, clean up this godawful mess before getting your asses to the PT bay by oh eight hundred hours."

Domino looked at his wrist, which didn't have a watch strapped around it. "What time is it?"

Major Winters glanced at his watch. "Oh seven twenty-eight." He gave the mess hall one more sweeping glance and shrugged. "That would be a tall order for any other soldiers here, but you aren't just any soldiers, are you? Figure it out."

Not wanting to give the pixies an opportunity to berate him for having interrupted the end of their private chow-time, Winters spun and marched back to the metal door. A few feet from the exit, he stopped, pulled a pen out of the breast pocket of his uniform shirt, and used it to scrape an unrecognizable glob off the sole of his boot. He then shoved the door open and disappeared into the hall.

Z and her cousins stared as the door swung shut, then reached up to tousle her short blue hair and sighed. "Huh."

"Major Winters turned over a new leaf." Domino grinned. "I knew he'd change his mind about us."

"He's not smart enough to do *that*." Z swept her gaze around the mess hall and pursed her lips. "He knows something we don't."

"That could be anything. Have you seen the guy? He's a freakin' Army dinosaur."

Echo fluttered down until she was four feet off the floor, not taking her gaze off the door. "We could always slit his throat in his sleep."

"Hot damn, Echo." Domino laughed. "Never stops with you, does it?"

"We wouldn't even have to draw sticks or anything." Her black wings made no sound as she rotated ninety degrees and set her black combat boots on the floor. She looked over her shoulder at Z and raised her eyebrows. "I'd be *happy* to do it."

"Yeah, I bet you would." Z shook her head. "I'm pretty sure slitting our new boss' throat would bring that stupid gnome back down on us, and he would ship us to Oriceran after everyone else."

Echo clicked her tongue in disappointment, although her expression didn't change. "*Please?*"

"Start cleaning." Z stood, spun her chair around and shoved it against the wall, and stalked across the enormous mess they'd made. "*Then* we can talk about what happens next."

CHAPTER TWENTY-ONE

It took the pixies all of five minutes to clean up the chaos in the mess hall and another fifteen minutes to find the PT bay Major Winters had mentioned. The facility in which they'd go through their OIP training was comprised of a series of halls and doors. Z thought it a test to see if they could find their way around without directions, but the man had left a trail of food footprints that were easy for the pixies to follow.

It only took her and her cousins as long as it did to find their next destination because the team had also left trails of food behind them when they'd left the mess hall.

Once they'd narrowed down which prints had been left by the major, the pixies followed those, although Major Winters had made a few stops along the way. When they turned down a hall with unmarked metal double doors at the end, multiple conversations, laughter, and shouts echoed toward them. Z figured that was where they were supposed to be.

She was right.

When she opened the doors, all conversation inside the bay stopped. Major Winters was standing near the Special Forces team, who looked like they'd been enjoying their time together without the presence of the three pixies.

The surprise on the major's face, either because the new recruits had found the PT bay without a map or because they'd managed to get here with ten minutes to spare, made Z smirk. *Bet he still thinks we're full of shit. Ball's in your court, Major.*

She waltzed into a room the size of a professional basketball court, spreading her wings wide to make sure everybody knew who she was. Not that there was much confusion.

"Hey, everybody," she called with a grin. "Are we late?"

Major Winters looked at his watch and scowled but didn't respond.

"Recruits!" he bellowed, still staring at his watch as his voice echoed around the bay. "Front and cent—" He looked at the pixies and pointed at a large black tape X on the floor. "Line up at the X."

Z and her cousins strode confidently across the bay, ignoring the equipment laid out for their first day of training. They focused on the soldiers standing a good ten feet from the X. Z and Domino flashed the team grins, and Domino lifted a hand to wiggle his fingers at them. True to form, Echo just swung her deadpan gaze from one face to the next.

The soldiers glared at them, but nobody spoke to the three recruits who'd made them look like idiots half an hour ago.

After the pixies lined up behind the black X, Z scanned

the PT bay. Blue and white lines ran around the perimeter of the room to form two lanes. Weights and exercise machines occupied the far-right corner of the room.

Behind Major Winters and to his right dangled a thick rope with knots every few feet that ended two feet above the floor. Black tumbling mats had been laid out inside the lanes at the back of the bay, and on them were a series of bars, ropes, platforms, and a swing.

Before Z could ask a smartass question about the setup, she was distracted by the sound of a dozen pairs of boots marching in near-perfect synchronicity toward her and her cousins.

The soldiers filtered out around and behind the pixies to form two straight lines, and Domino turned around to look at them. Then he returned his gaze to the major and pointed at the obstacle course. "Is that playground for us?"

"Recruits!" Winters barked without acknowledging the question. His eyebrows drew together as he addressed the pixies in the center of the front line. Though he hadn't overseen PT since he was a drill sergeant decades ago, drawing up the muscle memory for it was like riding a bike.

"For the duration of your training, everything you do will be observed and scored. By the end of this month, you should be able to meet the Army's standards for physical strength, acquire basic skill sets, use standard firearms and other weaponry, and, most importantly, work together as a cohesive team."

"We got *that* one in the bag," Domino muttered as he leaned toward Z. Though he'd lowered his voice to make it seem like a private comment, everyone heard it. "Guess he hasn't figured that out, huh?"

Z shot her cousin a quick glance, then returned her gaze to the major.

Winters ignored the disrespectful remarks and cleared his throat. "The objective of the Oriceran Integration Program is to train selected magicals in the tactics, strategies, skill sets, and mindset of a United States Army soldier."

He gestured at the lines of soldiers.

"Alpha Team's priority is to show you how things are done. These soldiers have been through it all, and if you're smart, you'll emulate them for the duration of your training. After that, you will apply the knowledge you acquire over the next month in a variety of combat situations, particularly those involving hostile magical entities."

Domino's hand shot into the air, startling the soldiers behind him and making Major Winters blink. When his CO didn't immediately call on him, he blurted, "What about the magic part? If you're tryin' to turn us into soldiers who don't use what their mama gave them—know what I'm sayin'?—what's the point?"

Winters stared at the pixie, then sighed. "That comes after the initial training." Then he realized his response had not been delivered the way a drill sergeant would have, so he added, "Interrupt me again, Recruit, and I'll smoke you up and down this bay until your feet bleed!"

"Ew." Domino looked down at his body and grimaced. "Like, in a pipe, or…"

"Two-mile laps, and you're timed. Move!"

The elite soldiers surrounding Z and her cousins leapt

to follow their orders. Several in the second line bumped into the pixies' arms and backs before taking off and forming another straight line. Then all twelve moved into the track lane and ran.

Z came close to shoving the last of them, which she could have done in her two-inch size, let alone at five-foot-five. She held herself in check because there would be an opportunity down the line to get her point across in a more efficient way.

Echo whispered in Domino's ear. "Yeah, tell me about it," he muttered as he glared after the soldiers, who were turning the first corner. "I was about to tell them how much better they looked *not* wearing their breakfasts."

Major Winters stared at the three pixies, who were still standing behind the black X. "What are y'all waiting for?"

They looked at him blankly.

"This isn't a demonstration, Recruits. Get your asses out there and run your two miles."

"You want us to *run*?" Z asked in disbelief.

The major growled, "What part of 'get your asses out there' do you not understand?"

"Yeah, about that." Grimacing, Domino jerked a thumb over his shoulder at the soldiers, who'd made it to the long wall of the bay. "We don't run."

"Not a thing pixies *do*, Major," Z added with a shrug.

"Are you fucking kidding—" Winters stopped, pinched the bridge of his nose, and took another deep breath. He straightened and glared at the banes of his existence. "You do now. I'm not running my mouth just to hear myself talk. When I give you an order, you follow it. *GO!*"

Domino wrinkled his nose. "Yeah, but *running*? Isn't there, like, something else we could do?"

"That's it!" Winters bellowed. "Drop and give me twenty!"

Z pursed her lips defiantly. Echo curled her fingers to study her nails and picked dirt out from under them. Domino glanced at the floor, then at his open hands, then cocked his head in confusion. "Twenty what?"

"For the love of all that is holy," Winters snarled through clenched teeth, eyes bulging from his head as he glowered at the male pixie. "You better tell me you know what a pushup is."

"Oh!" Domino's confusion disappeared, and his eyes lit up. "You should've said that, silly Major. But what am I dropping?"

"Your body on the ground!"

"Right." Domino nodded in understanding, looking like he was bobbing his head to a reggae tune. "That makes sense."

"*Now*, Recruit!"

"Okay, okay. Yeesh." Domino lowered himself to the floor to assume the pushup position. Keeping his arms, legs, and back straight, he craned his neck to look up at the major. "This means I don't still have to run, right?"

"Now it's thirty," Winters growled.

With Domino on the floor, Z and Echo had no one between them as they exchanged knowing looks. Z shrugged, then started to lower herself to the floor.

"What the— Blue! No." Winters pointed at the track. "You two, get out there. If you take a millisecond longer than ten minutes per mile, you're doing it again. Move."

Sighing, Z nodded for Echo to follow her to the lane. The team of soldiers had completed their first lap, and they kept running.

Domino started doing pushups, smiling as he moved up and down like he'd just unwrapped the greatest present in the world.

"How many laps do you think we have to do for two miles?" Z asked as she and Echo walked casually toward the lap lane, waiting for the last of the soldiers to run past them. Echo looked blank. "Yeah, forty should do it." She wiggled her eyebrows. "Wanna race?"

A tiny smile flickered on the goth's mouth as they stepped over the white line that created the inner lap.

Z chuckled. "You're on. Onetwothree go!"

Two sharp, loud pops echoed around the bay. Winters glanced over to see two streaks of light zipping around the perimeter of the room. One was gray, the other blue. "What the…"

Z and Echo caught up with the team of soldiers, who had a lap and a half on them, and zipped past them. The shockwave the pixies caused as they surged past knocked the closest men into their neighbors, and over half the team stumbled into the bay's walls with furious shouts and groans. Before they could right themselves, Z and Echo completed another lap and blew them back into each other.

The team paused to watch the glowing lines dart around the bay. The pixies were moving so quickly that they caught up with the end of the light trails around the room's perimeter and the glowing lines connected to make two rectangles of color.

Major Winters tried to follow the movement of the two dots creating the streaks, but he gave up after five seconds when dizziness and eye strain overwhelmed him.

Twenty seconds later, another loud pop echoed through the bay, and Z materialized in full human size where she and her cousin had begun their race. "Forty!"

Another loud pop followed, and Echo appeared in front of her cousin, facing Z with her arms folded.

"No, no." Z chuckled. "I didn't cheat. That was a close one, though. Hey, maybe *next* time, you'll beat me."

Z headed back to the black X on the floor. Echo flipped her cousin the middle finger without any change of expression and followed.

"Hey, Z!" Domino shouted from the floor. "Check it out. One hand!"

The pixie was completing perfect one-hand pushups using his right hand. He gave them a happy wave with his left.

Z clicked her tongue in mock disappointment. "Oh, come on. You can do better than that."

"Pinky?" His body continued up and down with flawless form, right elbow bending and straightening close at his side. The only parts of his body that touched the floor were the toes of his boots and the tip of his right pinky.

Z stopped a few feet away to form a triangle between her, Domino, and the scowling Major Winters. She wrinkled her nose and folded her arms. "I'm not impressed." Echo approached from behind and stopped beside her. "What do you think, Echo? Look like much of a challenge to you?" Her cousin did not reply. "Yeah, that's what I was thinking. Sorry, Dom. You are not *wowing* me."

Domino let out a low whistle as he continued to do pushups with his right pinky. He showed zero signs of tiring. "Tough crowd."

Major Winters remembered that he was supposed to have been counting the pixie's thirty pushups, but he had no idea how many had been done. He glared at Domino and barked, "Nineteen."

Domino let out a high-pitched giggle. "Somebody wasn't paying attention. This is forty-four, Major. Well, forty-five now."

"Still not impressed," Z murmured.

"Fine. You asked for it." When he pushed up, Domino put both hands behind his back and did hands-free pushups with perfect form. As he went up and down, he glanced at Z and Echo and wiggled his eyebrows. "Eh? How 'bout *no* hands?"

"Meh." Z shrugged, but she couldn't hide her smile at her cousin's mediocre presentation.

"Okay, look at this." He faced forward and stared at the floor as he lowered himself in a flawlessly straight pushup. "Watch the nose. What is that, an inch off the floor?"

"Hard to tell." Z bent forward as if she cared about getting a closer peek, then popped her head up to gaze at Winters. "What do you think, Major? That look like an inch to you?"

The ridiculous question ripped the major out of his bafflement. He blinked but didn't bother to answer as he scowled at Domino. "All right. That's enough."

"Fifty-seven," Domino said cheerfully as he continued his no-hand pushups. "Fifty-eight."

"Cut the bullshit."

"It's not bullshit, Major. These are gen-u-ine no-hand—"

"On your damn feet, Recruit!"

Domino paused halfway to the floor, then shrugged and straightened and stood squarely on the soles of his boots. He stretched his copper wings wide and shuddered, then settled them against his back. The pixie let out a contented sigh. "Now *that's* a workout."

Major Winters stared across the wide bay and muttered under his breath, "I'm not gonna make it through this."

Only then did he notice the dozen soldiers at the side of the room. None were running anymore. All were glaring hatefully at the pixies. One at the front of the line realized that Winters had noticed them, and he started jogging again. The others fell into line, but there was no point in demonstrating what running two miles in a qualifying period of time looked like for the magical recruits.

"Alpha, bring it in," the major called in a dejected voice.

The soldiers stopped their half-hearted jogging and fell into line around the pixies, still glaring. The three pixies just waited for the next task, ignoring Alpha Team's anger.

Domino nodded at Echo and Z with a self-satisfied smile as if he'd completed a vigorous mountain climb and been rewarded with a gorgeous view. "That was fun."

Z grinned. "Can't *wait* to see what comes next."

Major Winters tried to ignore them. "Moving on…"

CHAPTER TWENTY-TWO

The rest of their training that day in the PT bay wasn't any more successful than the beginning of it. Not in the traditional sense of Army training.

The rope climb lasted all of five minutes for all three pixies combined, who made it quickly and easily to the top. They celebrated each other's successes with cheers and applause, which were not offered by Major Winters or any member of Alpha Team.

Checking the pixies' calisthenics qualifications was a joke.

The obstacle course proved more interesting, but only because the pixies deviated from the demonstrated run. They used their vivid imaginations to make the obstacle course more challenging, but no one on Alpha Team could emulate their moves. No one on Alpha Team had wings.

The morning session Major Winters had planned for his new recruits, which should have taken four hours minimum, had been smashed down into an unorthodox hour by the Thornbrook pixies. Major Winters was running out of ideas.

He went with something he was sure would be another epic fail, thanks to the pixies, but it would buy him time to think. "Sergeant Lindon."

"Sir."

"These recruits need a lesson in command drills. You're drill sergeant for the team."

"Yes, sir." Lindon stepped away from the straight line of soldiers, spun to face them, and stared straight ahead as he asked, "How long are we running drills, sir?"

Major Winters eyed Z and her cousins. "For as long as it takes to get it right, Sergeant."

"Yes, sir!" Lindon lifted his chin, straightened his back, and dove into his new role as the OIP drill sergeant. That was the last thing a highly trained, qualified, experienced Special Forces soldier could expect to be. "Alpha Team, ten-*hut*!"

The elite team stood at attention as if they'd gone back to Basic Training. They glared at their stand-in drill sergeant since they knew what was coming. Given how Z and her cousins had taken on every task since signing their lives over to the OIP, they all knew how long this would take.

And how much it would suck.

When eleven pairs of boots clicked their heels and eleven soldiers stiffened to attention, Z turned to eye those in the second line. As it happened, Maass was behind her, staring straight ahead like a good soldier and refusing to look at the new recruit. She murmured, "This is gonna be fun."

"Alpha Team, right *face*!" Lindon called.

With the exception of the Thornbrook pixies, Alpha Team was the perfect unit for command drills. They carried them out a thousand times more crisply than any new-recruit platoon in history on their first day of Basic. None took any pride in their ability to perfectly perform command drills since this was not what they had signed up for when they'd joined the OIP.

It was humiliating, but they did it anyway.

Z and her cousins turned in slow circles and eyed the soldiers, snickering.

"Oh, *wow*," Z exclaimed, her eyes wide with delight when Lindon gave an about-face command, and the entire unit stepped back to put one boot tip on the ground before pristinely spinning a hundred and eighty degrees in unison. "It's like a remote control without the remote."

"Left *face*!"

Alpha Team turned their backs on Sergeant Lindon.

"Wait a minute." Domino wagged a finger from side to side as he drew a map of the last few commands in his head. "Is it just me, or did they just do a zigzaggy circle?"

"I like zigzags," Z murmured.

"Seems like a lot less work to turn around the first time. Lindon's gonna wear his voice out if he keeps screaming extra directions."

Echo whispered in her brother's ear. "Totally. I assumed you had to test at a certain IQ before they let people just, you know, play with weapons. Guess not."

"Alpha Team, forward *march*!"

The eleven elite soldiers did as they were commanded

since following commands was their job. Liking them wasn't.

The echoes of their crisp march across the bay, stepping in rhythm without any stragglers, made Z smirk. The soldiers who'd stood in line beside her and her cousins took off without waiting for the pixies to catch up or looking over their shoulders to egg them on.

Alpha Team had marched off the bay toward the metal double doors, leaving the pixies behind.

"Whee! Look at 'em go!" Domino gave the soldiers an enthusiastic round of applause.

Z spun to face Sergeant Lindon. "Do they roll over and play dead too?"

Lindon ignored her and bellowed, "*Halt!*"

The soldiers stopped immediately, the front line standing inches from the bay's doors and the rear line two feet behind them, with a three-body gap in the middle.

"Hmm." Domino tilted his head and stroked his chin. "You know, I can't help but think there's something missing. Those lines would look a lot nicer if there wasn't all that space in between. Right?"

"Totally." Nodding, Z pretended to think of a way to fix the problem. "Hey, Major Winters! Can we do something to fill in that gap over there? It's a real eyesore." She spun toward Winters with a coy smile. "Maybe you could pull a few extra soldiers in here to…"

She scanned the far end of the bay, pausing to look for movement on the obstacle course. She didn't find any since the only other person on that side of the room was Sergeant Lindon.

Major Winters was gone.

"Sneaky, Major," she murmured.

"About *face*!" Lindon barked.

Alpha Team turned as one.

"Forward *march*!"

Beneath the echoing crack of eleven pairs of boots marching in perfect time back across the bay, Z met her cousins' gazes. "Looks like the major took a break."

Domino pursed his lips in contemplation. "We're here for how long?"

"As long as it takes." Z smiled. She couldn't help her surge of enthusiastic joy at the perfect opportunity that had been presented to them on a silver platter. "He just never said what that is."

They glanced at Echo, who lifted a thumb and drew it across her throat.

"Huh." Shaking her head, Z pretended to think about what her cousin was insinuating. She chuckled as the soldiers of Alpha Team kept marching toward them. "As long as it's all in good fun, right?"

Domino rubbed his hands together. "Bring on the *training*."

CHAPTER TWENTY-THREE

At 11:58 a.m., Major Winters left his break room and headed down the hall to the PT bay. Before he'd stopped in front of the metal double doors, the sounds of three pixies' high-pitched laughter and nonsensical shouts came from inside, punctuated by Sergeant Lindon's shouted commands and the perfect clip of eleven Special Forces soldiers forced to run drills "for as long as it took."

Winters didn't reach for the doors' handles. He clasped his hands behind his back, turned around, and headed back to his breakroom for another cup of coffee and the ham sandwich he'd packed early this morning. The unorthodox but brilliant plan he'd concocted to get three unruly pixie soldiers to fall into line and take things seriously had been set in motion, and it had taken him all of twenty minutes to prepare. He would just sit back, wait for the Thornbrook pixies to do their part, and watch what happened.

If those twerps didn't take this seriously by lunchtime, maybe they'd get the picture before dinner.

Though he didn't relish the idea of ordering a team of

SF soldiers to run command drills with three magical nightmares holding up the show, it was part of the process—most of which he was making up as he went. All the same, he couldn't help but smile as he strode casually back down the hall, whistling a random tune.

He knew what was coming, hopefully by the end of the day, and when Major Winters had a plan in place, he was as patient as they came. The major's faith in the new magical recruits had apparently been too much since when he returned to the closed doors of the bay at 5:00 p.m., the noises coming from inside hadn't changed. The only exceptions were that Sergeant Lindon's voice was hoarse from shouting command drills nonstop for eight hours and the ragged breathing from eleven chests as the rest of Alpha Team demonstrated their excellence even when their orders in this new, highly aggravating, secret Army side program were not the best.

The pixies were still hooting and cackling, their voices switching from human timbres to the high-pitched squeakiness of their two-inch forms. Since those voices moved around within, Winters figured the little punks were flying as they shouted insults at the soldiers and tried to goad Alpha Team into breaking ranks.

Eight hours of drill hadn't crumbled Alpha Team's resolve.

Therefore, Winters left the PT bay again since his stomach had started to fold in on itself. Fortunately, being the OIP commander didn't require him to babysit twenty-four-seven. When 8:00 p.m. rolled around, the major made a final trip through the facility to the PT bay. The noises from the other side of the double doors had changed.

There was silence within.

That's too damn quiet. As soon as he had the thought, babbling whispers and hushed giggles made their way through the doors. The pixies were still at it.

The major's gut tightened when he realized that could mean anything in regard to Alpha Team. Eleven men who'd done exactly what he'd commanded, and he'd left them alone with the delinquent little devils for eleven hours.

Unsupervised.

Unchecked.

Unprotected.

Not that there was anything Winters could have done to protect the twelve-man team from three pixies with magic and an insatiable appetite for pissing everybody off, but still.

Shit. If I don't count twelve breathing human bodies in there, that gnome better fucking show up, stat.

The major grabbed a handle, jerked it down, and shoved the door open like he wasn't terrified of what he'd find on the other side.

It wasn't twelve massacred Special Forces soldiers, but it was far from reassuring.

Sergeant Lindon was standing in the same spot as when Winters had left the bay, arms down at his sides, chin lifted, and mouth open as if he were about to shout one more command. However, no sound came out, and the sergeant didn't move even when his CO stepped into the room.

The rest of Alpha Team was motionless in the center of the bay, formed into two straight lines with a three-man gap in the middle of the rear line as they faced their acting drill sergeant in this pitiful excuse for a training exercise. Though their posture was erect and alert, arms flush against their sides and fingertips pointing straight down the way they'd been trained to march years ago, something was very wrong.

It took him a few seconds to figure out what that something was. When he did, white-hot rage flared inside him so quickly that he couldn't move.

Each member of Alpha Team looked frozen in their endless command drill because they *were*. That was the only thing that made sense because it wasn't possible that eleven elite soldiers could stand on one foot, opposite knees bent and slightly raised as they prepared to step forward again, without moving a centimeter.

No trembling muscles. No twitching fingers. No wobbles, nor did he see the slight lowering of the raised leg that occurred when even highly disciplined individuals attempted to stand still for more than thirty seconds.

Alpha Team hadn't recruited statue performers off the streets.

When Winters pushed past the rage and could form full sentences, he searched the bay for the three insubordinate shits he knew were responsible for this. He couldn't find them until he heard a giggle from near the ceiling.

"Oh, *hi*, Major," Domino called in the chipper voice that bordered on flirtatious half the time. "Good to see ya."

The pixies hovered in a circle beneath the bay's high ceiling, their legs crossed beneath them. They looked like a trio of grade-school kids who were ready for storytime.

Z broke into the wide grin Winters had already come to

loathe. "Not very nice to take off like that without even saying goodbye. Guess you're a busy guy, huh?"

Domino let out a knowing chuckle. "That doesn't excuse giving us the slip. You were gone for so long, we thought you'd forgotten about us."

Echo said nothing, but she did sprawl out, folding her hands behind her head, her back turned to the major.

Z and Domino gazed at Winters expectantly. When the major didn't speak—since he was struggling to comprehend what he was seeing—Domino asked, "What's up?"

Trembling, Winters clenched his fists and snarled the first thing that came to mind. "What the fuck did you do to them?"

"Who?" Z looked around the room, then gasped and pointed at the frozen Alpha Team. "Oh, you mean those guys. We froze 'em." She spread her arms. "Figured that was obvious."

Gaping at the frozen team, Winters shook his head. "What made you think that was a good—"

Domino interrupted. "It got so *boring*. Back and forth and back and forth, and all the yelling, you know? Like, 'Okay, we get it. You can stop screaming.'"

Z nodded sagely as if her cousin had delivered an eloquent philosophical theory. "Plus, they looked tired, Major. Started to feel bad for 'em, you know? I hope this isn't the only thing you expect us to do for the next month. The repetition's a real buzzkill."

Winters clenched his fists, fighting to keep his composure. The damn pixies had taken it way too far, but unfortunately, not far enough. If they had, Carmine would have popped in to break the little devils' contracts and ship them back to their planet. *Where they belong. And here I am, trying to turn them into soldiers, for Chrissakes.*

He glared at the pixies and growled through clenched teeth, "Fix it."

"You sure?" Z asked with concern. "I don't know if those guys can handle another minute of marching."

"Now!" The major's shout cracked across the bay, echoing with a ferocity he didn't recognize. He didn't recognize anything anymore, including his ability to successfully organize and implement the program.

His demand was met with silence.

When the pixies realized their CO wasn't going to say anything else, they gave in. With a sigh, Z flicked her hand at half the soldiers. Domino did the same toward the other half, and the frozen team was illuminated by copper and blue light. The eleven soldiers set their raised feet on the floor with a communal click of their boots.

Startled and baffled and disoriented by having been trapped by the pixies' magic, which, for most of them, was the first magic they'd ever experienced, Alpha Team groaned, stumbled out of their perfect formation, and gasped for breath.

Sergeant Lindon didn't move, and when they noticed, the rest of the team erupted in angry shouts and furious demands for the pixies to free him.

Z and Domino laughed, which got them an even darker glare from Major Winters. He didn't bark more orders at them, though.

"Okay, Echo." Z turned to her cousin, trying to look stern and reprimanding. "You made your point."

Still lying on her back in the air, the goth stared at Z for a few long seconds, then casually flicked a hand at the frozen sergeant who'd started the food fight in the mess hall with his anger issues.

A flash of gray light illuminated Lindon's body and freed him from the spell. Instead of shouting yet another command, the sergeant croaked in a hoarse, raw voice, "*Fuck!*"

Z clicked her tongue and shook her head. "So ungrateful."

"I know, right?" Domino folded his arms and pursed his lips as he eyed the disoriented soldiers, who were still trying to come to terms with having been frozen for the last hour. "Give 'em *one* magical break so they don't have to use their muscles, and they take a mile." Frowning, he turned to his cousin. "That's how humans say it, right?"

She shrugged. "Sounds good to me."

"Alpha Team," Major Winters shouted, shocked by what he'd walked into, "you're dismissed for the night."

As if they'd known this was coming, the soldiers stormed across the bay in a mass exodus, their perfect formation abandoned. None of them said a word, and they didn't look at each other as they exited, let alone at Major Winters standing right inside the door. As far as the pixies were concerned, the members of Alpha Team were acting as if the OIP didn't exist.

Mostly, they wanted to get the hell out of there, eat the protein bars or MREs they had stashed in their rooms in the facility, and pass out.

Sergeant Lindon was the last one to go toward the exit, and he was the only one to look at Winters, his lips pressed firmly together and his eyes narrowed with rage.

Winter managed only a weak nod, and Lindon slipped through the bay doors. They swung shut.

Now it was only Winters and the Thornbrook pixies, and it seemed like the Army's three new troublemakers had run out of smartass comments. That didn't last long.

With an expectant smile, Domino floated down to hover cross-legged three feet off the floor. Then he spread his arms. "So, how'd we do on our first day?"

Winters spun on his heel, shoved one of the bay doors open with both hands, and stormed down the hall to his quarters.

Domino kept staring even after the bay doors clanged shut again. "Huh."

Z floated down to join him, though she uncrossed her legs and landed with her boots on the floor, then clapped his shoulder. "I'd say it went pretty well."

"Could've used more bloodshed," Echo muttered dryly, still lying on her back in the air.

Her cousin and brother burst out laughing.

CHAPTER TWENTY-FOUR

As they went to the quarters they'd been assigned, Z and her cousins joked about what a great time they'd had during their first day of OIP training. None of them felt bad about what they'd done to Alpha Team or the impression they'd left on the soldiers and Major Winters.

They were pixies, and those beings didn't care about anything unless they had a good reason to do so.

As far as Z and her cousins knew, they had no good reason to care. None of them had any idea that one such reason was waiting for them in their quarters.

It didn't take long.

"And his *face!*" Z exclaimed as she shoved open the door, spun to face her cousins, and walked inside backward. "It was like he'd just watched us kill his puppy."

Domino chuckled, then straightened and pulled off a semi-accurate impersonation of the major. "'As long as it takes.' Ooh, so *scary*, Major. Wouldn't wanna do anything to waste your precious time."

Without moving her head, Echo gazed around the bay

as she walked toward the circle of bunks that hadn't been touched since they'd left at 5:00 a.m. That was because no one wanted anything to do with the pixies' private space. "Pathetic," she said flatly, then flopped on one of her bottom bunks and stared at the underside of the one above her.

"You gotta admit they try *really* hard. Poor creatures." Domino raised both arms above his head and dove onto his combined bunks, making them shudder and squeak.

Z snorted and made her way toward her bunks to join them. She stepped through a space in the circle, then grabbed the metal edge of the top bunk she hadn't used yet. "They're trying *too* hard."

Her cousins glanced at her curiously. "What do you mean?" Domino asked.

With a shrug, she kept her gaze on the edge of the bed frame, tightened her grip, and leaned back to stretch her arm. "Mostly Winters. The guy's got something to prove, that's for sure."

"Oipcamp," Domino replied, then he and his sister snickered at the ridiculous name Echo had coined.

Z smiled, but her mind remained on Major Winters and the niggling feeling that she'd missed something important. She couldn't put her finger on it, so she replayed their first day in her mind: putting on their uniforms, hitting up the mess hall for chow, the food fight they hadn't instigated but had finished, Winters telling them to clean it up.

"That's it," she muttered, then straightened, grabbed the frame with her other hand, and leaned back.

Domino frowned at her from his bunk. "Yeah. I just said it."

"There was only one time today when Winters looked like he was in control. When he *smiled*."

Her cousin shrugged. "Maybe we broke him."

Echo pounded a fist in her opposite palm. "I'll break him more if you want."

"There was something off about it," Z continued, ignoring her cousins. She now had a few pieces of a puzzle she didn't understand, and it took concentration to put them together.

I know I'm missing something...

"Hey." Domino sighed. "You look like you're starting to take this seriously."

Frowning, she whipped her head toward him, and her concentration melted in a snort as she released the bunk's frame. "Right, because being a US Army pixie is all I've ever dreamed of."

Domino chuckled, and a smirk flickered across Echo's lips.

"I mean, it does have a few perks," he added.

His sister pounded her fist again. "Like breaking humans."

"True." Z sat on her bunk and leaned forward over her lap. Whatever she'd been about to put together about Major Winters' strange response in the mess hall was fading.

She didn't have enough pieces to put it all together yet, and if something wasn't crucial to solving a problem, a pixie didn't spend her time worrying about it. "It's better than the other crappy option they gave us," she added. "Would've been nice if some of the others had stuck around for a little longer."

"Who?" Domino clicked his heels together, and the next second, his Army-issue boots were on the floor by his bunk instead of on his feet. "Calinda and Co.?" He snickered. "More pixies equals more fun, right?"

"We should go steal all the humans' shit and burn it," Echo murmured.

Z and Domino turned to her in silent admonition, and the goth held their gazes. Then she shrugged and returned to staring at the underside of the bunk above her.

Z lay back on her bunk to stretch her legs. "We had some fun times with those guys, huh?"

"Loads." Domino waved his finger, and a line of copper light followed the movement. He drew Major Winters' scowling face and added a shiny red clown nose, then floated his magical art into the center of the bunk circle. "I miss those guys. Had a hell of a run with 'em, and you know what? If I had to pick the best job, I'd pick the last one we pulled."

"Nope." Echo rolled her head to stare at her brother. "I didn't get to punch anybody."

"Hey, don't put that on me." Domino lifted both hands. "That's on you."

"It *was* a good last job," Z agreed. "Even if we had no idea it was gonna be the last." The bay fell silent again as the pixies remembered their old crew and the hundred years they'd spent running and stealing and wreaking havoc with Calinda's gang. Then an excited grin of realization shattered her contemplation. "Speaking of that last job…"

She rolled off her bunk, caught herself with a flutter of

her wings, and dropped onto her knees in front of her storage drawer.

When she didn't finish the first part of her thought, Domino rolled onto his side and propped his head on one hand. "Spill the beans."

"Remember that envelope I found in the safe deposit box?"

Her cousin's expression morphed into disappointment. "You're excited about a human's piece of paper. Awesome."

"It was definitely more than that." Z looked up at him as she pulled the drawer open. "It had an Oriceran symbol on the front. Some kinda old magic, except there wasn't any magic on the envelope."

"Ooh." Domino raised his eyebrows, now interested. "A human stashed Oriceran letters in his secret box with his extra cash and watches? *That's* weird."

"I know. I didn't get a chance to open it before Alpha Team started blowing up our— " Z peered into the drawer. "*What!*"

Domino snorted. "That's what *I'd* like to know."

The open drawer into which she'd placed her personal belongings this morning was empty.

"Z. Come on. The suspense is killing me."

"I like suspense," Echo added. "Especially when it comes before—"

"It's gone," Z growled.

"What, the letter?"

"All of it." She reached into the empty drawer and felt around, banging her hand against the metal sides and bottom since someone could have cast an illusion on the contents. But there wasn't any magic here. Her stuff was gone.

"What do you mean, *all of it?*" Domino asked. His voice was serious.

"I mean all my fucking things, Dom!" Z slammed the drawer shut, then assumed her pixie size and zipped across the bottom bunks toward the opposite side. The other bunk's storage drawer clanged open, and blue light flickered into the center of the bunk circle as the horrified pixie bounced around inside the drawer. "Shirt, jacket, pants, sneakers. I put them in the drawer, and they're gone."

Domino and Echo glanced at each other, then turned their focus to the drawers beneath the bunks they'd chosen. After quick flicks of their hands, their prospective drawers opened. The siblings shrank and scanned every inch of their storage spaces.

"No!" Domino shouted as he flung open his other drawer. When that didn't produce the results he wanted, he darted toward the bunks' bottom mattresses and surged under those. Both mattresses leapt from the frames and flew across the bay, then slid across the floor. Both mattresses from the top bunks followed suit, and he zipped around, leaving a trail of copper light. "No, no, no, no!"

Though she hadn't thrown the mattresses off her bunks, Echo searched her spaces just as thoroughly and came up with the same result. She did, however, punch the metal frame in front of her. An ear-splitting screech filled the bay when the bunk scraped across the floor under her blow. Then it bumped noisily against the far wall and was still.

Breathing heavily, Echo stared at the empty air where

her bunk had been and seethed. "I told you we should've slit his throat in his sleep."

"Fuck." Still two inches tall, Z fluttered into the center of their bunk circle. She settled onto the floor, then her wings shuddered once and drooped against her back. Her unfocused gaze settled on a dark scuff mark on the floor, and she took a long, deep breath. If she didn't calm down before her rage flared and made her do something that couldn't be undone, their one chance to stay on Earth and avoid Oriceran would be gone.

I promised them we'd never go back. Think, Z. There's a better way to handle this than losing my shit and tearing this whole place down.

Domino settled down on the floor with her, though he landed on his stomach with his face on the floor and his wings drooping over his limp arms. "What kind of monster would *do* that?" he moaned, his voice muffled against the floor.

Z stared blankly at nothing until the reality of what had happened hit her. Then she *knew*. "The kind of monster who thinks he's smarter than us," she snarled.

"Monster." Echo landed on the floor with two light thuds and spread her arms. Fiery vengeance glowed in her eyes. "Let's kill it."

That made Z glance at her cousin. "I'm talking about Winters."

The goth blinked. "Same difference."

"Winters?" Domino pushed off the floor enough to flop onto his back and lay there like an empty shell since that was how he felt. "Why would *he* want our stuff? None of it'll fucking fit him."

"He didn't take our things because he *wants* them," Z interjected as she shot her cousin a scathing glare that wasn't aimed at him. Domino didn't take it personally. He never did. "He took it all to keep us in line."

"Monster," Echo repeated. She looked at Z and nodded. "Let's go find him. See how *he* likes it to have his soul stolen."

"Yeah." Her brother perked up. "Right out from under him. Or in him? Dammit, where do humans *keep* their souls?"

"Like I have any idea," Z snapped. Her cousins understood that her anger and sharpness had nothing to do with them. If Major Winters was here, he'd bear the brunt of her rage, but he wouldn't have handled it as well as they did. They knew how their cousin operated.

They waited for her to make a decision since they couldn't let this slide.

"It's my fault." Z shook her head. "He wanted to look through our stuff for those scissors we never took, and I stopped him. Shit, I wasn't thinking when I drew that line. I handed it to him on a silver platter. 'Hey, here's our biggest weakness. Strip of us who we are since that's the only way you'll have anything on us 'til you set us loose."

A morose, helpless silence fell over the bay.

Then Z felt a shimmer of weightless magic and looked up to see a glowing silver smiley face with lopsided lines hovering in front of her. Echo's attempt to cheer her up wasn't as effective as getting back their personal belongings. Those were the things that made a pixie unique among thousands of other two-inch flying magicals. The things that showed on the outside who they were on the inside.

She stared at the smiley face, which drooped more to one side the longer it hovered. She laughed wryly and shot a glance at her cousin.

Echo didn't attempt to emulate her drawing's reassuring smile, but she did raise her eyebrows. "The human took what's ours. *He's* the monster, Z. Not you."

"Yeah, but *I* promised to keep us all safe." Z sighed and shook her head. "I got us out of a one-way ticket back to Oriceran, but now…"

Domino shrugged. "Now we have nothing to lose besides breaking our magical contracts and getting sent to some shithole on a planet we hate by a wrinkled old gnome who hates *us* almost as much. But hey, who's counting?"

Her cousin's spirits were lifting, but Z still felt guilt and anger and determination. She wanted to harness the pixie optimism that had gotten them out of tight spots before, but it was harder this time. She was sitting in a military facility wearing military clothes without anything to call her own.

Without anything that made her *her*.

Our things aren't gone. Winters kept them to use as carrots. He doesn't wanna destroy us. He just needed to find the right motivation.

"I didn't think he had enough brain cells for that," Domino added. "Surprise, surprise. Point is, it's not your fault."

Z raised an eyebrow and pursed her lips.

"Honest." He raised a fist, looked at it, and tried to form the shape he'd intended with his fingers before shaking his head and giving up. "You said it yourself. You got us out of Oriceran, and you've *kept* us out. You'll figure out a way to get back what belongs to us *and* make sure we get to stay."

"I kinda like this planet," Echo muttered, then gave a half-hearted shrug with one shoulder. "Even *with* all the humans. I guess."

"It's better than where we came from," Z agreed. "That's for damn sure."

"Totes." Somehow, talking it out had mostly returned Domino to his chipper self. He rubbed his hands together and wiggled his eyebrows. "So, what's the plan?"

"The plan." Z took a deep breath, straightened her shoulders, and lifted her chin. Her blue wings fluttered back to life at her sides. "The plan is we get our things back, whatever it takes."

Domino nodded, ready and willing to follow her to the end like he always had.

Echo tapped her lips. "Before or after we slit his throat?"

"Sorry, E." Z managed a smile that felt natural and real. "You're gonna have to wait a little longer on that one."

The goth rolled her eyes and spun toward her bunk like a moody teenager, then fluttered onto the mattress. It was far too big for her natural size. "I hate waiting."

They all did, but they were willing to do whatever it took to get back their possessions. They now had something to care about and a reason to light a fire under their asses.

That was now their mission.

CHAPTER TWENTY-FIVE

The next morning, Z and her cousins were on their feet with their bunks crisply made, the semi-destroyed bay put neatly back together, and their Army uniforms on and ready to go. There was nothing they could do about the slits in their shirts, and Echo wasn't going to return her all-black attire to camo, but Z figured Major Winters was not very concerned about his magical recruits looking like every other soldier in the Army.

The man wanted his pixie trainees to fall into line so he could call his ridiculous new program a success, so that was what they'd give him.

When Winters realized that, the real fun would begin.

Starting with the baffled look on the major's face when he threw open the door and stormed into their quarters, ready to yank the pixies out of their bunks. He found all three standing at attention, waiting for their CO to speak.

It was too much to comprehend, and the man froze. The bay door squealed as it banged shut behind him.

He glanced at his watch to see that it was 4:58 a.m. as

he'd thought, then cleared his throat. It took him a few seconds to figure out what he wanted to say, and he scanned the face of each pixie before he came up with the option that sounded the least ridiculous. "Chowtime, Recruits. Move."

"Yes, sir," the pixies chanted in unison.

For the first time in his Army career, multiple voices giving him the appropriate response made the hairs on the back of his neck stand on end. He couldn't let it go.

No way in hell did they have a change of heart. These aren't the same shits who tried to give me an aneurysm yesterday.

His frown deepened, then he remembered that this was what he'd been hoping for.

You took their stuff, Henry. This is what having leverage looks like, remember?

His confusion lifted, and Winters produced a cold, devious smile. "I thought you would have more than *that* to say this morning. Something happen?"

Z lifted her chin and glared at the major, though she emulated Echo's blank face so she wouldn't give anything away.

He divined that she was burning to spit something out, so he clasped his hands behind his back and gave her a curt nod to test these uncharted waters. "Permission to speak freely, Blue. Go ahead."

"You know exactly what happened," Z replied, her voice low, unwavering, and tightly constrained despite the venom in it. "Sir."

"Huh. Maybe I do." Winters nodded, feeling prouder by the second as he directed his gaze from one uniformed pixie to the next. "Looks like y'all finally decided to get your shit together. Not gonna lie; it's a good look." His gaze settled on Echo, and he eyed her all-black OCPs. "Except *that*, but sometimes we have to make concessions before we come to a mutual understanding. Compromise, if you will. I'd say that's where we are. As long y'all don't fuck up anything else."

Z wanted nothing more than to launch across the bay, grab the man by the throat, and shake him until he told her what he'd done with their things. Instead, she stood still and silent between her cousins and let the major's goading wash over her.

You're playing the long game now, Z. Deal with it.

"I'm glad you agree," Winters added and nodded. "Now get to chow. You're dismissed."

Without another word, the pixies headed toward the bay doors behind him. The major watched them intently, thinking one of them might lash out as they passed.

He clearly had nothing to worry about right now since the three broke away from each other to march around their CO and slam through the metal doors.

Then they were gone.

Winters stood there for a moment, hoping he'd made the right call and terrified that he had taken things too far. His terror didn't last long since he'd given the three biggest thorns in his side a simple command, and they'd carried it out as if they'd been doing it for years.

The doors' *clangs* freed the major from his confusion. He scanned the empty bay one more time, let out a happy chuckle, and went toward the hall to see what else he could get the Thornbrook pixies to do.

How long would their sudden, albeit resentful, obedience last?

Z and her cousins had no trouble finding their way through the labyrinthine hallways to the mess hall. Since they'd started their day at the appropriate time, they reached the entrance to the mess hall at the same time Alpha Team did.

Neither party stopped, turned, or slowed as they converged on the open doors from different directions, but Alpha Team's glares were impossible to ignore.

Anyone else in this situation would have buckled under the tension and animosity filling the air. That was often the cause of fights between new soldiers barely finding their feet in the Army and their careers.

However, Z and her cousins weren't "anyone else." They'd had more than a century of practice ignoring things that would have distracted them if they hadn't been on a side mission. They would play the game until they tracked down their belongings and retrieved them.

That would take time, but pixies had plenty of it. Compared to humans, they had all the time in the world. The Thornbrook pixies were not expecting to use more than the month allotted to them for their special program training. Hopefully, less than that.

They marched into the mess hall with the soldiers of Alpha Team, effortlessly avoiding the broad shoulders swinging their way in vengeful attempts to trip them.

Just keep playing the game, Z. Play it until they all let their guard down. Then you'll have the chance to do your thing.

Alpha Team was still holding a grudge. Nobody said anything, but it was clear they despised the pixies for putting them through yesterday's ordeal.

Z and her cousins were aware of their hatred, but pixies didn't care.

When Winters stopped by the mess hall at 5:47 a.m. to see how the trick up his sleeve was working, he was pleasantly surprised to find all twelve members of Alpha Team and the three recruits sitting quietly at the four tables. What didn't surprise him was that the dozen soldiers had commandeered three of those tables, so the pixies were forced to sit at the fourth on their own.

No one was tossing spiteful or inflammatory comments across the room, and the food stayed on plates and platters and in mouths where it belonged.

With a self-satisfied smirk, Winters gave himself another moment to view the calmness in the mess hall, which he hadn't expected to find on Day Two.

He'd engineered the OIP to last only thirty days instead of the traditional ninety of regular Basic Training. Apparently, his decision to fast-track magical recruits had been the right way to go, even though he'd spent the day before thinking that he'd made a serious mistake. He'd assumed that any magical who agreed to enter the program would be the same as the droves of human recruits in Basic Training.

Convinced that they were on the right track, Winters left the mess hall and returned to his break room, where he had an enormous cup of gourmet coffee and a burrito from beyond this facility's walls waiting for him. Alpha Team and their CO saw the same new attitude in Z and her cousins when they assembled in the PT bay to continue what they'd started yesterday. None of the soldiers expected that they would *finish* what they'd started today, but the Thornbrook pixies proved them wrong.

Z, Domino, and Echo were the perfect soldiers, falling into formation with Alpha Team and completing every command drill as if they'd been doing it for as long as the human soldiers. The pixies' change of heart and the soldiers' surprise at their shift lessened the Alpha Team's glares.

Winters made them run drills for the rest of the day to cement his point with the rogue pixies, but he dismissed the unit for both lunch and dinner, which did even more to boost morale.

That didn't mean that the Thornbrook pixies became fast friends with the elite soldiers, but they didn't have to. They only had to do their jobs well enough and long enough to finish their personal mission under everyone's noses.

Though the content of their training changed, the pixies continued their new behavior through the next day in much the same way, and the next, and the next. Overnight, Z and her cousins became model recruits.

During hand-to-hand combat training, they watched and learned and soaked everything up without interrupting or making a mockery of it. When they sparred with Alpha soldiers so they could put those new skills to use, none of the Thornbrook pixies held back.

No one had ordered them not to use their wings or

their magic since a military training program for magicals didn't make much sense if they couldn't.

Nine times out of ten, Z, Domino, and Echo beat their opponents. The only reason they lost any bouts was that Lindon had taken it upon himself to fight dirty.

Every time he was paired with a pixie, he went straight for the wings. That was the one thing that tripped the pixies up. He did acquire two black eyes and a grotesquely swollen split lip because of it, but that didn't keep the sergeant from smiling, which he did a lot despite the pain it caused.

After that came weapons training and firearms qualifications. Echo was tempted to turn the standard Army rifle she'd been handed on various members of her new unit, specifically Sergeant Lindon and Major Winters, but the warning stares from her brother and cousin reminded her of why they were doing what they were doing. Thus chastened, she aimed the barrels of her various firearms at the appropriate targets, scowling as she fired.

Domino discovered a love of live ammunition when he found out he could flick a round at his intended target with as much speed and accuracy as if he'd loaded a weapon. Since launching a round from his fingers instead of a standard-issue firearm wasn't forbidden, he used the magical method on the indoor firing range more often than not.

Z scored high on her weapons qualifications too and maintained her marks from the beginning of their training to the end. The only member of Alpha Team who could hit the center of his target more consistently and faster was

Corporal Emerson, who took every opportunity to rub it in her face.

Under different circumstances, Z would have made it difficult for him to say much for the duration of their training, but she held herself in check and kept practicing. She did not, however, acknowledge the man's slightly better skills.

CHAPTER TWENTY-SIX

During the first three weeks of OIP training, Z, Domino, and Echo did everything as ordered and expected. Some of the soldiers forgot the recruits weren't human—until they stood behind the pixies and got a view of the glittering wings protruding from the slits in their OCP shirt. Then their fellow soldiers had to roust them to get them to stop staring. Over time, however, it happened less frequently, and the fifteen-soldier unit was finally able to focus on bigger and better things.

Like getting through what for some had become Hell Month so they could finish the damn training and go their separate ways.

On the outside, the Thornbrook pixies were becoming acceptable Army soldiers with an extra and unique punch. However, while they fooled everyone else involved in the OIP, they were taking note of everything around them.

At night, when Major Winters and Alpha Team assumed the pixies were asleep, Z and her cousins roamed through the facility's twisting hallways, which were lined with countless secured rooms. They gathered information to bring them closer to fulfilling their personal mission.

They learned that the facility where they were being trained, which was restricted and hidden so they couldn't step outside into the fresh air and warm sunshine, was near a place called NORAD. Domino thought it was a stupid name. Z told him to shut up about it when they went out to scour the facility for clues about their stolen belongings, but he couldn't let it go.

They learned that NORAD had been built inside a mountain in Colorado close to Fort Carson, which was a regular Army base, and went on forever in multiple directions. That factoid could have been a major problem, but Z was convinced that Major Winters wouldn't have taken their carrots miles away to keep them from being repossessed.

She was certain the man would keep his only leverage close. Possibly in his quarters, where in the night, he could set a hand on the pile of things that didn't belong to him to reassure himself of the power he held over his magical recruits and slip quietly back to sleep. That was what she imagined, which compelled her to search Winters' quarters first.

Her cousins had no problem with that, and the three of them dove back into their old habits of breaking and entering, with a side of theft if they were lucky.

Slipping under the door's crack into the major's room had been easy. Winters, for all his grumbling and groaning when the pixies took things too far for comfort by melding magic and military tactics, slept like a log.

A snoring log.

Domino had a difficult time holding back from creating mischief inside the major's room. While Z and Echo silently searched the bare desk and its drawers, the bureau filled with neatly folded clothing, and the man's toiletries, which were neatly laid out or stacked in the small but functional bathroom attached to his quarters, the copper-winged pixie had an undeniable desire to wreak havoc with the major's sweet dreams.

He lasted as long as it took for his sister and cousin to scour every inch of Winters' room. When they zipped back into the center of the room, Domino's willpower broke.

He hovered over the major's face, holding one of the man's boots over his head as he fluttered back and forth in pixie size. The end of one loose shoelace dangled inches beneath that boot and trailed across Winters' eyes, nose, and mouth, tickling the man enough to make him snort and flutter his eyelids in his sleep but not enough to wake him up. That would have ruined all their efforts.

When Z saw what her cousin was doing, she couldn't believe he'd deviate from the plan like that. However, a pixie with a plan was still a pixie.

"Dom," she hissed, hoping to get his attention without further disturbing Winters' sleep. "Cut it out. We gotta go."

"Just a little longer," he protested. He snickered when the plastic end of the shoelace snagged the major's nose hairs.

Winters snorted louder, then his mouth popped open. His next inhalation was a loud snore that made Domino flutter up two inches.

Z grimaced at the close call, but fortunately, the major hadn't woken. "I'm serious," she hissed, shooting toward her distracted cousin. "Are you trying to screw this before we find where he put our stuff?"

"No." Domino's tongue poked out from between his lips in concentration as he lowered the end of the shoelace onto Winters' face again. "I'm *trying* to get him to slap himself in the face."

"You gotta put something in his hand for that," Echo muttered as she studied the major's empty hands. "Like fake blood."

"What?"

The siblings were talking too loud for this to end well.

"Keep it down," Z whispered harshly. "You're gonna wake him up."

Echo tilted her head. "That toilet in the communal bathroom's been clogged up for, like, four days. You could pull something outta there and stick it in his hand."

Her brother's eyes lit with excitement and he shouted, "That's *perfect*!"

Winters' snore cut off, and he shifted. The pixies froze, waiting to confirm whether he'd roll over and go back to sleep or if they'd disturbed him enough to wake up.

When it was clear that the major was a heavy sleeper, Z shot a warning glare at Domino and pointed at the boot in his tiny hand. "We're leaving. Drop the boot."

"Aw, come on, Z," he whined in a whisper. "This is what we *do*."

"Not until we're whole again, it's not."

"But it's so—"

"I said, drop it." She hadn't intended to infuse her magic into that hissing command, but it happened.

A bolt of blue light burst from her outstretched finger,

zapped the major's boot, and crackled over the black leather exterior. It didn't stop when it reached Domino's fingers.

"*Ow!*"

He dropped the boot and shook out his magically electrocuted hand, and the footwear plunged toward Major Winters' face.

None of the pixies could move fast enough to stop it.

The boot hit Winters' cheek and temple with a thud. His snore turned into a croaking shout of pain and surprise as he thrashed beneath his sheets. "What the—"

Z and her cousins sped out of there before things got worse.

Three streaks of light headed for the crack under the door. The gray and copper streaks slipped into the hall first, closely followed by the blue streak.

"Goddammit!" Winters shouted as he sat fully upright and rubbed his temple. Groggy from being rudely ripped out of a deep sleep and distracted by the pain in his face, he scanned the dark room with a half-lucid scowl, then looked at the ceiling to find the cause of his midnight attack.

Z took that brief window of opportunity to point at the boot, which had toppled onto the floor. A tiny sliver of blue light raced across the room, barely an inch off the floor, and knocked it toward the chest of drawers to join its twin in a straight and upright position.

Though he heard the thump of that boot settling back into place, Major Winters couldn't for the life of him find out what had made the noise. He grumbled a little longer, rubbing his face, then turned over and instantly fell back into a deep sleep. He never found out what had caused him to wake at 1:48 a.m. three weeks into overseeing the first round of OIP training.

Fortunately, he was too far gone to hear the pixies cackling as they raced down the hall toward their quarters.

CHAPTER TWENTY-SEVEN

Z had to weasel a promise out of both cousins that there wouldn't be any more funny business until they found their things and figured out how to get them back. Making a request like that of any pixie was an exercise in futility. However, Domino and Echo weren't blind to how close they'd cut it in Major Winters' private room, and they respected their cousin enough to agree to what she was asking. They wanted the same thing she did.

So, they came to a mutual agreement and were surprisingly successful at sticking to their promise. In the back of her mind, though, Z had a feeling that sooner or later, somebody was going to notice the bumps and clangs and shushed whispers moving through the halls in the middle of the night. They were running out of time, and they hadn't gotten any closer to finding their stolen belongings.

For the next three nights, the pixies scoured every hiding place they could think of, searching a multitude of rooms within the facility. Putting themselves into the mindset of Major Winters, however, proved difficult.

On the fourth night after the dropped boot incident, Z was almost out of ideas for places to look.

"There is *one* place we haven't looked yet," she told her cousins as they got ready to sneak out of their quarters.

Domino raised an eyebrow. "There's no *way* he got all our stuff into the sewer pipes. They were human-sized when he took 'em, Z. Also, you said he'd wanna give 'em back eventually. I know the major's not the smartest pickle in the bottle, but he wouldn't forget that he'd have to get our things *back out*."

Z stared blankly at her cousin, then sniffed. "I swear, Dom. Sometimes your brain goes to even weirder places than hers." She jerked a thumb at Echo, who shrugged.

Domino frowned. "Did you realize that was a compliment when you said it, or…"

With a snort, Z focused on getting her cousins back on track. "We haven't checked the holding room yet."

Echo rolled her eyes. "That's the worst idea you've had in, like, a hundred years."

"Oh, you're in an exaggerating mood now, huh?"

Domino scoffed. "Of *course*, we haven't checked it yet. We haven't gotten anywhere *near* the holding room, and you know why."

She did.

During their nighttime searches, Z and her cousins had given the hall that led to that room a wide berth. They had been terrified when they'd been stripped of their wings in that room.

Z had no idea how the old gnome had managed anything he'd done, including the disappearance of their wings. She *did* know he'd done something to the holding room to make it a threat to any magicals who entered Major Winters' new program.

Whatever was in, on, or around that room had taken away their magic, only to return it the moment they stepped into the hallway. That hadn't changed, and the Thornbrook pixies remembered the exhilarating rush of getting everything back. None of them wanted to lose it again.

They'd stayed away, but they were nearing the end of their month of training. Winters might not return what he'd stolen, and they'd run out of options.

"It's the only place left," Z noted.

Her cousins' fearful stares didn't make her feel any better, but they had to give it a shot. "Listen, I know you don't wanna go there—"

"No shit," Domino muttered.

"I'd rather gouge my eyes out with Lindon's big toenail," Echo added. She gazed at the ceiling in thought and added, "Which sounds fun as long as it's someone else's eyes."

Pressing her lips together, Z waited for her cousins' chatter to stop, which it usually did when she made the unamused face she was making now. It was the same look Z's mother used to give the three as kids when they were acting up too much even for *her* to handle, and it was very effective.

As usual, Domino broke first. "Fine. Go ahead."

Echo didn't respond, but she folded her arms, which usually meant she was willing to listen, however grudgingly.

Z nodded. "I know you guys don't wanna go there. Neither do I. That room gives me the creeps, and I'd love to burn it down." She pointed at Echo to stop her before the goth could add another distracting comment. "That doesn't mean you *can* burn it down, so forget about it."

Echo blinked in brooding acceptance.

"But think about it. Winters knows we want our things back. He knows by now that we've been good little soldiers because we're hoping he gives everything back at the end of all this, or at least he's noticed that we've been *acting* like it. I'm pretty sure that's the same thing to him."

Domino twirled his hand in a hurry-up gesture. "And?"

"And it makes sense that he'd put our things in the last place any of us wanna go. He might not know much about pixies or magicals in general, but he knows magic is integral to who we are, or he wouldn't have made an entire stupid program for training magicals. You can bet he hasn't forgotten that whatever the gnome did to that holding room, it's enough to keep us in check *without* our magic."

"You're putting a lot of faith in one puny human's understanding of magicals," Echo said. "I still vote for slitting his—"

"You guys trust me, right?" Z looked at her cousins, raising her eyebrows and searching their faces.

Though Domino frowned, he didn't disappoint her. "You know we do."

Echo nodded, which was enough.

Rolling her shoulders and stretching her wings, Z pointed at their quarters' doors. "Then that's where we're going tonight. If I'm wrong, you guys can call the shots when we try again tomorrow night."

"Deal!" Domino stuck his hand out and grinned.

She raised an eyebrow. "We don't need to shake on it."

"Yeah, we do. That's how deals are made."

"I got warts on the entire right side of my body the *last* time we shook on a deal. I know you remember that."

He kept holding his hand out for a moment, then dropped it. "Fine. It wasn't gonna be warts anyway."

Z turned to Echo to make sure both of her cousins were on the same page about this. "You in?"

Echo said flatly, "Whatever. We're all gonna die anyway."

Domino snickered. "Yeah, in, like, a thousand years, give or take."

The goth raised an eyebrow. "That's what *you* think."

The pixies headed out for the straightforward next step in their personal mission. None of them *wanted* to get near the magic-dampening holding room, but that didn't matter.

The halls were silent and empty, as usual. Z and her cousins darted down the halls and around corners as glowing orbs, leaving trails of light behind them.

Given how quickly and efficiently they'd learned to navigate the confusing series of hallways over the last few weeks, it was easy to find the holding room. It would have been difficult to avoid it if they didn't know where it was.

The itch on Z's back was the first sign that they were entering the range of the room's magic. She hadn't felt that since they'd recognized the hallway for what it was, and a brief surge of dread filled her as she flew closer beside her cousins.

We're not going into the room. I think. Even if we have to, nobody's here to shut the door on us and lock us in. This is just a recon mission. If we have to regroup and modify our strategy, fine.

It didn't occur to her how much military terminology she'd picked up and was using in her thoughts. Pretending to be a soldier hadn't been that different from being one, but her mind had been on other things since the end of their first day.

A few feet down the hall, Domino pulled up, raised a hand to his forehead, and clenched his eyes shut. "Whoa."

Z saw that he'd fallen behind and turned around so as not to leave him behind. "I feel it too. You okay?"

He shook his head, groaning, then took a deep breath. "I think so."

"Last one there has to go in first," Echo called from farther down the hall than Z expected. "Whoever it is, I volunteer to close the door on you to see what happens."

Z and Domino exchanged glances, then darted after her, trying to cut the head start she'd gotten.

In no time, they were there.

Even if the pixies hadn't recognized the hallway and the outer walls of the room, they would have known they didn't want to be here.

The feeling of their magic, their very essence, being slowly drawn out of them toward some unseen center was a hundred times stronger. Z's stomach churned, and she wondered if she might vomit. She realized the holding room's door had been left open.

Narrowing her eyes and swallowing against the magically induced nausea, she asked, "Didn't Winters close that door when he took us out?"

Domino's eyes were glassy as he stared through the open door. "Can't remember."

"No clue," Echo added.

Major Winters had had more important things on his mind than closing the door to a room laced with intensely strong magic he couldn't feel, so he might not have. If the door *had* been closed after she and her cousins had walked down this hall, however, then it had been opened again—and there was a good chance that it had been opened to bait three pixies into sating their curiosity about what was inside.

"I guess it doesn't matter," Z murmured before swallowing again. An uncomfortable burp made its way up her throat, but that was it. "Can either of you see anything from here?"

"Just the floor and the walls," Domino replied thickly. "Maybe death."

The pixies exchanged nervous glances, then Echo fluttered forward and peered in. She took great pains not to touch anything in case the enchantments that had taken away their magic were flowing through the walls and door and floor of the room.

"Mirror. Table. Chairs. Just like before," she murmured. Squinting, she leaned farther forward, but she fluttered back when she saw a reflection in the mirror. "Shit."

"What?" Z flew up behind her cousin but didn't get too close. When Echo was in a tense situation, coming up behind her was like walking right behind a spooked horse.

"Please tell me it's something good," Domino pleaded.

"No." Echo pointed into the magic-dampening room

and looked over her shoulder at them. "But our stuff's in there."

"For real?"

With a shrug, Echo moved aside and gestured for her cousin to have a look. Z flew to the open door and leaned forward like her cousin had. She scanned the parts of the room she could see, and the giant mirror on the far wall caught her eye.

In it, she saw a tall, narrow metal locker that had been brought into the holding room after the pixies had been released. It wasn't a standard locker with a solid metal door and sides that hid its contents. This locker had narrow metal bars, and she could see shelves inside.

Z recognized her bomber jacket and the red toe of one of her sneakers on the middle shelf. The bottom shelf was crammed with black items, and the top held a bundle of dark-green corduroy.

White-hot rage flared inside her, and she made the mistake of leaning too far into the room as she thought about going after the locker then and there. Having the top of her head in the dampening room and the rest of her body out in the hall made her feel like she was being torn in half, and she reeled away and turned to her cousins.

They were waiting for her to decide what they would do.

"It's all in there." She clenched her fists. "Locker just around the corner."

"Let's go get it." Before his sister or his cousin could hold him back, Domino darted forward in a blurred streak of copper light. He made it inside before the room's dampening effect caught up with him. Two inches of male pixie became a five-foot-eleven human-looking man without magic or wings.

His forward momentum and increased size sent him stumbling forward to crash into the steel table in the center of the room. Chairs clanged into each other and toppled over, and the table skidded across the floor with a grating screech.

Domino sprawled on the table with his legs dangling over the sides.

"Dom?" Z asked, fluttering as close to the doorway as she dared. "You good?"

He groaned. "What part of this looks like I'm good?"

"If we had scalpels," Echo muttered, "it'd look like one of those tables where the humans cut up their dead, but you'd have to be dead first."

Domino pushed up, slid off the table to stand beside it, and glared at his sister. "How come you never don't talk when it's just the three of us?"

She didn't speak.

"While you're in there…" Z added, hoping he'd pick up on the rest.

He did, but not before he pointed at her. "You're gonna owe me after this."

"Only if you get our things out of there."

Rolling his eyes, Domino stomped across the room toward the locker. Z fluttered backward to check up and down the hall. Though they'd spent weeks sneaking out every night to look for their stolen things, tonight was the first time they'd made noise. If they were seen here, it was game over, but she wasn't going to tell her cousin to stop.

If any Army personnel came down this hall to find blue

and gray lights hovering in front of an open door, Z and Echo could probably distract them long enough for Domino to get their things and get the hell out of there.

It was a decent contingency plan.

Until Domino rattling the door to the locker echoed into the hall, followed by a hiss of frustration. "Damn."

"We don't need a play-by-play," Z called, shifting her eyes between one end of the hallway and the other, "but a quick summary would be nice."

"It's locked."

Echo rolled her eyes. "Oh, *no!*"

"We can bring lockpicks," Z offered. "We've done it before."

"It's an electric lock. You know, where you put your finger on it or your eyeball or something. I can't get it open."

With a sigh, Z approached the door again and fluttered to the right angle so she could see both her cousin's human-sized back *sans* wings and a sliver of the locker with their stolen belongings. "Then just grab the whole thing. We'll get it open, no problem."

"It's bolted to the floor," Domino informed her. "So that's a no-go."

"Shit." She searched her mind for anything that might work in a situation like this, but all of them required the use of magic, which was not something they had access to inside the room. Besides, Carmine Ratchetter's magic was much stronger than anything the Thornbrook pixies could rustle up.

"Okay, come on out. It's brainstorming time."

Domino left. As soon as he passed through the open

door, he stumbled and almost crashed into the opposite wall. His copper wings returned, as did the inebriating effects of having all his magic returned to him at once.

With a giggle, he leaned against the wall. "That was *fun*."

"We need ideas. Lots of them. So let's—"

"Race ya back to our quarters!" Domino shouted in his human voice. Then he became a two-inch copper orb and darted down the hall, cackling.

Echo zipped after him, quickly gaining speed. Z followed her cousins back to the sleeping bay, encouraged that they'd finally found Winters' hiding place. They didn't have that much time until their training ended, and they didn't have much experience in burglary *without* the use of magic.

We'll have to step up our game. Shouldn't be a problem.

CHAPTER TWENTY-EIGHT

Completing their side mission turned out to be a lot more complicated than Z had expected since she and her cousins had to think like humans, which was difficult and weird and confusing. A pixie could look human if they wanted to, but getting into the headspace of a non-magical expert at breaking and entering didn't come easily.

They had to improvise.

Their first plan of attack included attempting to get to the metal locker from *outside* the room. Z and her cousins combined and blasted streams of attack magic that would cut through any substance on Earth. As soon as their pixie-magic saw cut through the first layer of drywall covering the holding room's outer perimeter, their plan backfired.

The gnome's protective magic reacted to the attack like it had reacted when Riverly had tried to open the door from the inside. Jagged crackling lines of electric-blue magical energy shot from the wall, eating its way up the pixies' combined attack and throwing them across the hall.

Singed and thwarted but full of raw determination, they tried twice more with the same result.

After that, they tried less drastic approaches. Z thought they might be able to find Major Winters' fingerprints around the facility, more specifically in the major's quarters. Dom volunteered to go in and look for the prints, but after the boot-dropping incident, Z shot that down.

"I can go cut off his thumb," Echo suggested.

Z clicked her tongue. "Yeah, leave this one to me."

To her surprise, searching for Winters' fingerprints on the doorknob, walls, desk, bathroom counter, and everywhere else she could think of was futile. After two hours of scrutinizing every surface and coming up empty-handed, Z slipped back under the major's door to rejoin her cousins.

"So, how'd it go?" Domino asked with a grin.

"Nothing." Z zapped the piece of Scotch tape she'd taken with her to capture said fingerprints, and the tape burst into a million fluttering fragments before disappearing.

"Nothing?" He snorted. "Who doesn't have fingerprints?"

"Maybe someone cut off all his fingers, and he's got fake ones now," Echo murmured.

Z scowled and shook her head. "I think he did it on purpose."

"What?"

"Cleaned off all his fingerprints."

Domino grimaced. "Don't you think the major would've said something if he knew we were on to him?"

Z thought about what she knew of Major Winters. "Nope. I don't think he'd say anything."

Their final attempt to get into the barred locker in the holding room used Domino's suggestion. Z and Echo were apprehensive about letting him take the lead, but he was adamant that he could make it work.

"Remember the last time?" Z asked as they sat in the circle in the center of their bunks. "They were finding squirrels in the Louvre for *weeks* afterward."

"Yeah, but that wasn't *my* fault." Domino grinned. "I showed them the way out, but the squirrels *wanted* to stay. Pretty sure that's not gonna happen here."

"They keep nuts in the Louvre?" Echo asked.

Domino shrugged. "Some kinda peanut exhibition, I think. You know, art and stuff."

Finally, Z signed off on her cousin's unorthodox plan to get their things out of the locker, and he rushed off to do his thing.

When he returned half an hour later, he was escorted by an entourage of mice that were ready and willing to do his bidding.

"You said you only needed a few," Z chided as the critters surrounded her and Echo. "This is two dozen."

"Well, I can't help it if they *all* wanna be a part of a secret mission." Domino walked beside a large mouse in the way a rancher would walk beside a horse they were leading. He lovingly scratched behind the mouse's ear, cooing, "Isn't that right, Crumble? Who's a good boy? Crumble's a good boy, that's who. Yes, you are."

Domino's ability to befriend and conscript a wide variety of critters was the only reason Z had entertained his idea, and it had seemed like this particular plan would work. Z and Echo flitted down the hall toward the holding room with a pack of field mice scurrying after them. Domino, who was grinning like a lunatic, was riding Crumble into battle at the head of the mousey horde.

He had to dismount when they got to the holding room since riding Crumble through the door would have resulted in a human-sized pixie atop a flattened mouse.

"Okay, guys." He eyed the mice in turn. "You know the plan. Go do your thing."

He delivered a loving slap to Crumble's hindquarters, and the mice headed into the holding room. The clicks of their tiny claws were deafening to pixies small enough to ride mouseback, but to other Army personnel, it would just sound like a rodent infestation. Fortunately, the sound didn't carry far.

Unfortunately, someone had done their homework on the pixies' previous exploits and hidden mouse traps around the room.

So intent had Domino been on investigating the locker that he'd failed to notice the traps and their redolent bait tucked into the corners of the room. By the time the pixies noticed the trap that had been set for them, it was too late.

The sharp claps of four mousetraps engaging in quick succession filled the holding room, followed by the rest of the mouse squad's terrified squeals and skittering claws as they abandoned their directive and made a swift retreat.

Domino gasped and clapped both hands over his mouth, moaning, "Oh, the *horror!*"

The pixies darted away from the stampede in time to avoid being trampled, and Domino urgently searched the scurrying bodies. "Crumble? Crumble, where are you? Has anyone seen Crumble?"

A sharp, agonized squeak came from inside the room, and Domino darted inside. The second he entered the room, he was just over five feet tall. He fell onto his knees and skidded across the floor to the far corner. The wailing Crumble had only gotten his leg caught and nothing else, fortunately.

"I gotcha, buddy. Don't worry. I gotcha." After gingerly scooping up the wounded mouse and the trap, Domino hurried out to the hall and set his precious cargo on the floor. Then he shrank to pixie size and blasted copper light at the trap, which broke apart to release the mouse's rear leg.

Crumble slid out of the mousetrap and lay on his side, staring at the three pixies looming over him, his sides heaving in pain and terror.

"Come on, Echo." Domino gestured at the wounded mouse. "Help him out."

She stared at the creature, then pointed. "It's still alive."

Z nudged the goth with an elbow. "Don't be a jerk."

Rolling her eyes, Echo stepped toward the frightened animal, knelt beside him, and swiped her finger across his injured leg like she was wiping dust off a shelf. Silver light raced across Crumble's leg, repairing shattered bones and shredded tissue.

When the light faded, Crumble wriggled onto his feet and let out an appreciative squeak.

Domino patted the mouse's head and nodded solemnly. "I know, buddy. I know. We lost some good mice in there. I'll never forget their sacrifice. This I swear to you."

Crumble snorted, then scurried away to rejoin the mice retreating through the halls and walls.

For the next twenty-four hours, Domino didn't say a word to anyone.

The pixies continued training in human size with Alpha Team, excelling in field exercises. Using their magic to complete the drills, the FTX objectives, and create mischief among the unit—though nothing nearly as detrimental as freezing a dozen soldiers and holding them in suspension—made following orders much easier.

It never occurred to the pixies how odd it was for the OIP training to be completed indoors. They couldn't compare it to normal Basic Training, which was mostly held outdoors, nor did they know that the experimental training program wasn't close to seeing the light of day. To top it off, the United States Army wasn't ready for the OIP or its first three magical recruits.

The rest of Alpha Team grew accustomed to the new recruits' eccentricities and irritating quirks, and the shouted insults from the first few days became nicknames of acceptance.

Z, Domino, and Echo became Blue, Peter Pan, and Tinkerbell, though the humans refused to explain who the fairytale characters were despite Domino's frequent and increasingly urgent demands to know why anyone would name a pot *or* a pan.

Even Sergeant Lindon had softened to the irksome trio, though he would never have admitted it.

Z and her cousins spent their days being good recruits and their nights trying everything they could think of to get to that locker in the holding room, break it open, and retrieve their things.

When magic had proven fruitless, the pixies turned to methods more frequently used by humans. Their discovery of the tool room produced a slew of new ideas for breaking out their personal belongings, but the pixies had no idea how to use hammers, wrenches, or screwdrivers. All proved useless after hours of banging the locker's metal bars and bio-security lock with them.

They eventually had to give up because of the noise. Domino giving himself a black eye with an Allen wrench was the last straw, though the injury was grudgingly healed by his sister. It occurred to Z how odd it was not to have sounded any alarms during the noisiest of their endeavors, but she had a feeling there would be no attempt to catch them in the act. It felt like the major *wanted* them to make a spectacle of themselves since he expected them to fail.

Eventually, Major Winters granted them twenty-four-hour access to firearms like every other soldier on Alpha Team. They could fetch what they needed during their training exercises themselves, but they were responsible for returning the weapons at the end of the day. That had been done for them until they earned the trust required to do it.

Shortly thereafter, they were put on fire guard duty to roam the facility's halls at night while everyone else was asleep, an activity that required full combat gear and weapons.

Z and her cousins made quick work of slipping into the armory after hours to try using the various military-grade weapons on the seemingly impenetrable locker. To their disappointment, none of the weapons was loaded, and Winters was smart enough not to keep live ammunition in the armory. Banging on the metal bars with handguns and rifles wasn't any more effective than using human tools.

They almost ruined their chances of retrieving their belongings or passing their month-long training to keep up their end of the deal with Major Winters when Echo had finally had enough.

In the middle of their fourth and final week, Z and her cousins made one more attempt at breaking out their personal items, but when they reached the holding room's door, Echo was nowhere to be found.

Z darted up and down the hall in a ball of blue light, growing more anxious by the second. "She was right behind you, wasn't she?"

"I thought so."

"Then why isn't she here?"

Domino shrugged. "Hey, I'm not her babysitter."

"Well, go back and find her. If someone sees her flying around in the middle of the night… Wait." Z cocked her head and heard footsteps steadily approaching. "Someone's coming."

"Right now?" Domino spun in circles to search the hallway. "Why would anyone else be…"

He didn't finish the sentence since the sight of his sister rounding the corner at human size knocked all other thoughts out of his mind.

Echo had gone for one of the big guns—a large, intimidating rocket-propelled grenade launcher that was almost as big as she was. Her pixie strength allowed her to carry it as if it weighed nothing, although how she'd gotten hold of a grenade with the ammo under lock and key was a mystery.

"Echo," Z hissed. "What the hell are you doing?"

"What we should've done a long time ago," the goth murmured.

Domino chuckled nervously. "You're not really going to use that thing. Right?"

"Echo?"

The pixie marched down the hall, stopped in front of the holding room's outer wall where the locker was on the other side, and took aim.

Z zipped toward her cousin and flitted up to the launcher to study the attached and ready-to-fire grenade. Her eyes widened, and she grabbed the end of the weapon to jerk it forcefully to the side. "No!"

"Go hard or go home, right?" Echo ground out, fighting Z's efforts to turn the weapon away from the wall.

"That doesn't apply to this!" Z shouted. "Do you want the old gnome coming back here and shooting *you* with a grenade? No! Fucking put it away."

The idea of being shot by Carmine made Echo pause. She stared at the wall she'd intended to blast, glanced at the weapon in her arms, and heaved a massive sigh. "Then I'm out of ideas."

She dropped the launcher and shrank before racing down the hall.

Fortunately, Z and Domino were fast enough to catch the weapon before it clanged on the floor and caused more trouble than they could handle. After sharing a horrified glance, they slowly and carefully returned the launcher to the armory, and because they'd learned how to load and empty all the weapons they'd trained with so far, they emptied the large weapon before calling it a night.

It was hard to work out what to do with the grenade since the rest of the ammunition was locked up, so they found an unused locker at the back of the changing rooms and stowed it there. With any luck, it would stay there and gather as much dust as the space containing it.

After that, Z and her cousins teetered on the edge of giving up.

"It's not gonna work," Domino moaned as he lay flat on his back in their quarters. "I don't know how he did it, but the major made it impossible."

"Nothing's impossible," Z shot back, though she didn't sound certain even to herself. "We just have to keep trying."

"We'll *die* trying." Echo gave an airy sigh. "There goes the rest of my life."

"Don't do that." Z shook her head. "Don't give up."

"What choice do we have?" Domino added, looking crushed. "We're just shells now, Z. That's it. He's gonna hold us hostage by keeping our things in that room forever."

"No. I won't let that happen." She meant that, but she had no idea how she was going to make good on it.

CHAPTER TWENTY-NINE

With two days left of their training, Z and her cousins weren't any closer to freeing their belongings. Any attempts they might have made on the second-to-last day were thwarted during one of their training exercises with Alpha Team in the enormous underground field room.

The pixies and a third of Alpha Team's soldiers were completing their mission objective—to cross the room under "enemy fire" and infiltrate the "enemy base" on the other side. The room was set up like a laser-tag arena, with obstacles and areas of cover the teams could use.

Following Bixby's hand signals to go around one of the physical obstacles with two other soldiers and flank the enemy base, Z crouched and made eye contact with Echo. They shrank to pixie size to zip toward the next location.

The alarm went off.

The blaring siren drowned out everything else. Alpha Team dropped out of the exercise since every human soldier understood what that alarm meant, even if their pixie colleagues didn't.

"Everybody out!" Lindon shouted. "This is not a drill! Let's go!"

The team emerged from their hiding places and raced out of the training room, falling into a neat line as they did.

When they burst out the open doors, they discovered the hallway beyond filled with thick smoke that made it impossible to see anything beyond the next few feet. It obscured their only way out.

"Keep moving! Follow my voice!" Lindon commanded.

The pixies raced alongside the soldiers, and Z realized she and her cousins weren't as disadvantaged as the rest of the team. "Dom! Echo! Come on!"

Her cousins sped toward her, their silver and copper lights illuminating the smoke as they caught up with the blue glow.

"What the hell do you think you're doing, Blue?" Lindon called after them.

"Saving your asses!" Z shouted, darting ahead with her cousins on either side. Once clear of the soldiers, she stopped in mid-air and let out a blast of force energy that cleared a corridor through the thick smoke.

Domino and Echo did the same, and by the time Alpha Team caught up with them, they'd cleared enough smoke for the team to find the closest emergency exit. It was in a location the Thornbrook pixies had not been privy to during their month here.

Lindon stopped beside the three bobbing orbs of light and looked the pixies over. "Neat trick."

"Not if we don't get out of here and away from the fire," Z muttered. "Not a lot we can do with *that*."

"Then let's keep moving." He glanced at the rest of the team. "Keep close and move fast."

The pixies stayed beside him since they had no idea where they were going. Working together, they managed to clear the smoke enough for the sergeant to see every branching corridor they encountered on their way out. Alpha Team moved through the halls in a bubble cleared of smoke, staying close and following the soldier in front.

When Lindon turned down one of the halls, the itchy, gut-churning feel of the magic-dampened holding room hit Z like a train. She hesitated, but the soldiers kept moving into the smoke.

"This sucks," Domino murmured. "Where the hell's the fire, anyway?"

"Does it matter? Let's go." Z led her cousins down the hall, using bursts of magic to clear the smoke so Alpha Team wouldn't suffocate or get lost.

When they passed the open door to the holding room, none of the soldiers noticed it or one very different, very important detail. Z raced past the open door and saw it when she shot a quick glance at the mirror.

The locker was still there, but the door hung open as if waiting for her to grab her things and run.

Domino and Echo had fluttered past her, neither wanting to spend more time near the magic-sucking room than necessary. They hadn't seen the open locker and were busy blasting back the smoke to get the soldiers to safety under Lindon's shouted directions.

It's a trap. Or a test. Z smirked at the mirror. *This whole thing is a test. I could race in there right now, lose all my magic, and grab everything.*

"Blue!" Lindon shouted from down the hallway. "Where the hell are you? We need all three of you to clear this hall. Let's go!"

Gritting her teeth, Z raced past the open door, her chest tightening at the realization that she'd come close to regaining her freedom.

It wouldn't really be freedom, would it? She and her cousins would get their things back, but they would have abandoned their team during an emergency—even if that emergency was a simulation.

When she'd passed the holding room, she was certain that was what Major Winters had expected from her and her cousins. It sucked.

She reached her cousins, who were fluttering at the edge of the smoke in front of Sergeant Lindon. Lindon shot her an irritated look, then the pixies blasted away another ten feet of thick, stinging smoke so the team could follow without being asphyxiated or running into unseen obstacles.

A moment later, Lindon shoved open a door at the end of another hall and stumbled out into bright sunlight and fresh air. Alpha Team barreled out behind him, coughing and gasping for breath and hauling their choking fellows out of the facility.

Z and her cousins hardly noticed that they'd spilled out into fresh air for the first time in a month. They were focused on pulling the last of the soldiers out of the hall as billowing smoke spilled out the open door.

The team figured it was safe to take a break and let themselves bask in the fact they hadn't been burned alive or choked to death on the smoke.

"Everyone here?" Lindon called, scanning the soldiers standing or sitting or lying on the grass. He did a quick count, then nodded. "Fifteen. Good."

"What about Major Winters?" Maass asked and started hacking. When he'd recovered somewhat, he continued, "Lemme tell ya, when he said to go with the fake fire, I didn't think he was gonna use *actual* smoke."

"Gotta make it feel real," Bixby added, then doubled over, propped his hands on his thighs, and took a deep breath. "Would've been nice if he'd left gas masks lying around."

"What, you mean you can't breathe smoke like the rest of us?" Brakeman shouted, and the team burst out into raw laughter interspersed with coughs.

"Uh, Z?" Domino sidled toward his cousin. "Do humans hallucinate in emergency situations?"

"Maybe some of them." She smiled. "But I don't think that's what this is."

The alarm blasting inside the facility shut off, and a deafening silence fell on their surroundings.

Ten seconds later, Major Winters walked around the corner of the building with his hands clasped behind his back, his face an unreadable mask. He scanned the team on the grass and the three pixies hovering together to one side. "I'd call this mission successful."

"Jesus Christ," Bixby muttered. "I'm never touching another cigarette."

Alpha Team chuckled, but Z didn't hear them. She was focused on the major's knowing smile and the brief dip of his head acknowledging the Oriceran Integration Program's magical recruits.

Z realized they'd just graduated.

Four hours later, the Thornbrook pixies knocked on the door of Major Winters' breakroom and received a curt "Enter."

Exchanging wary glances with her cousins, Z opened the door and poked her head in. "You wanted to see us, Major?"

"Yep. Come on in." He gestured at the empty seats in front of his tiny desk. The furniture barely fit the room and made the small space crowded. Despite that, the pixies filtered into the room.

"Take a seat."

They obeyed. Sitting down was easier than asking the major what this was about.

He swept his gaze from one pixie to the next, then folded his hands on the desk. "I honestly didn't think this was going to happen. I thought the three of you would tear this place down rather than successfully complete your training. But you did complete it."

He didn't sound too happy as he spoke, and it didn't help that his frown deepened with each word. "So now I have to figure out where the hell to put you."

Echo whispered in her brother's ear. Domino nodded at the major. "She says something in demolition would be cool."

Winters choked on his next breath but tried to cover it. "No way."

Z snorted and couldn't help smiling. "You're saying we passed."

"Yeah. I guess that's what I'm saying. Great news, huh?" There was no ignoring the sarcasm in the major's response, especially when he added, "Congratulations."

He surprised them again when he grabbed something off the floor on his side of the desk and lifted it with both arms to reveal a clear plastic crate containing familiar gear. Watching them carefully, he plopped it on the desk. "Figured that might be enough of a reward for now."

Z beamed when she recognized her bomber jacket through the clear plastic. "That'll do."

She stood to grab their things from the container, but Winters interrupted her by thrusting a hand toward her.

"Y'all exceeded my expectations, which isn't saying much, but still. Welcome to the Army."

Z shook his hand, followed by Domino and Echo. Then the pixies grabbed the crate and went through their things, holding favorites to their chests.

"Anything else?" she asked.

"Not currently, no. Your job now is to stay out of trouble in this facility and wait for your new assignments."

"Right." Z cast her cousins a knowing glance and added, "I'm pretty sure we can handle that."

"Mostly, yeah," Domino added.

"Super." Winters didn't sound impressed, but he nodded at the door. "Get out."

The pixies hurried toward the door but stopped.

"Uh, Major?" Z glanced over her shoulder. "Do you mind?" She raised her armload of personal items, inferring that all their hands were too full to let themselves out.

Rolling his eyes, Winters stepped out from behind his desk to fulfill the seemingly harmless request from the Army pixie. He had to squeeze past them to get to the door, and when he reached Z, she stumbled into him in her attempt to make more room.

"Watch it,"

"Sorry, sir. Still dizzy from all that smoke." She fixed him with a sheepish smile, but he frowned and opened the door.

"When I say wait for your next assignment, that's exactly what I mean. No funny business."

"Yes, sir," they echoed as one before filing back into the hall.

The door slammed shut behind them, but Z and her cousins were unfazed. They had their personal effects back because they'd shaped up and played the game the way it was meant to be played.

Z, however, had something else as well.

After they'd turned down two more halls on their way to the sleeping bay, she pulled an extra item out of the pile of her clothes and dangled it in front of her cousins. "Hey, guys. What do you think I should do with this?"

Her cousins eyed the identification badge hanging from her hand. It had Major Henry Winters' name and clearance level on the front.

Echo grinned.

Domino burst out laughing. "You're freaking insane. I wish I'd thought of that!"

"Hey, he took something from me. I'm taking something from him."

"How long are you gonna hold onto it?"

They kept walking down the hall, and Z shrugged as she slipped the identification card back into the pile of her clothes. "Eh, couple months should do it."

Echo whispered in Domino's ear. "She says five bucks he starts squirming about it after a few hours."

Z chuckled. "Deal."

Get sneak peeks, exclusive giveaways, behind the scenes content, and more. PLUS you'll be notified of special **one day only fan pricing** on new releases.

Sign up today to get free stories.

Visit: https://marthacarr.com/read-free-stories/

AUTHOR NOTES - MARTHA CARR

WRITTEN FEBRUARY 1, 2023

I've started a project answering questions for my son about my life. I realized after last year's fifth round of cancer, and then chemo this time that he was expecting me to die sooner rather than later. It's been a lot for him to deal with and there isn't much I can do to make it better, except tell him stories that I can leave behind – eventually. Hopefully, a long time from now. I'm going to let you guys listen in as well.

My author notes for this year are going to be answers to questions and all of you can get to know me better, too. Maybe inspire, maybe give you a laugh along the way.

Today's question is: Did you move when you were a kid? What was it like?

We moved twice when I was growing up. The sum total till I was an adult and found it difficult to stay in any one spot for very long. I went through that long phase in my fifties of going on vacation with everything I owned. I was a little late to wanderlust but it was totally worth it. I taught myself that I'm resilient and adapt easily. Plus, I learned a lot about what I don't like, and then what I do.

But when I was a kid, there were seven of us altogether and Dad was an Episcopal minister. In the Episcopal church, it's more like a corporation with each level reporting to the one above it. Okay, I hear it. Also sounds like a multi-level marketing plan. I suppose that works too.

Anyway, the bishop has a say in who moves where and it has to be a church that can support such a large family and in those days, has a rectory (otherwise known as a house) that can fit us all. Not always an easy task. (These days they pay ministers more and let them buy their own house, and then also keep the equity. A better plan.)

We started out in Washington, Virginia, a tiny hamlet known for nothing back in those days at the base of the Blue Ridge mountains. It's affectionately called Little Washington to this day and now has a B&B that is known far and wide. It was a wonderful place to live as a very little kid. I could wander anywhere and had a million things to explore. Once a year I could stand at a window on the second floor of the rectory and watch the cattle be driven down the main street toward another destination. Once in a while on a hot summer day I had a nickel to get a very cold orange soda, my favorite. There were creeks and woods and wildflowers and dogs and other kids. It was a little piece of paradise.

But that job ended, and we all moved to the suburbs of Philadelphia. It was a brand-new house in a regular neighborhood, owned by the church. The first night the smallest of us ate pizza sitting in the new fireplace. It seemed like such an adventure. There were so many cars, and houses, and tall buildings, and that old ship, Old Ironsides, and smokestacks. Philadelphia was a very different place. At Christ Church, famous early Americans were buried in the aisle. It was considered a primo spot back in the 1700's. A lot of the cobblestoned streets were so narrow you would have thought it would be tough for one car, but they were two-way, the handles of each car passing each other with a breath's distance apart. The next-door neighbors, the Schraeders, had no children but a lush green lawn that they didn't mind my brother and I rolling across on a regular basis. The Dafts down the street would become our best friends, and Herbie across the street, and Herman up the street and Dot. There were so many kids and we could all roam free, without a tether at least until the street lights came on or someone rang a dinner bell.

There were also no fences so once you had to be home you could run the distance of the block, unimpeded, passing by everyone's house from the back. Everything was easier there.

But then that job ended too and we were off again. At the age of ten, we were all moved to a suburb of Washington, DC to the Virginia Seminary. It was an older house where the heat was tricky. My room went without heat for half the time I lived there. The elementary school was even worse. Leaking pipes, no heat some of the time, no air conditioning in the hot, muggy summers most of the time. And by middle school, there were regular riots started by someone from the nearby high school. And we didn't really have neighbors anymore, but other faculty members and their kids and all the politics that go with that sentence. That was a tougher place to grow up. But there were also amazing things like being able to always put together a last-second softball team or watching old movies on a classroom floor like The High and the Mighty, or the woods behind the house, or all the culture in DC.

But in my mind, Lafayette Hills, PA was the place that really nurtured me there for a while. Sledding down our street, trick or treating at every house, riding bikes everywhere. It's possible that it's mystique has grown in my mind, but I don't think so. It's gone now, anyway. All of the little ranchers have been torn down and the lots divided in two, replaced with two McMansions. Time moves on.

Now, I'm in Austin, Texas with my own home on my own little square plot of land with the gardens out back. I've done my phase of wandering and I can put down roots here because of my memories of Lafayette Hill, and because I really know what I want. Love you. Love, Mom. More adventures to follow.

AUTHOR NOTES - MICHAEL ANDERLE

WRITTEN FEBRUARY 1, 2023

Thank you for not only reading this book but these author notes as well!

This time, we tossed out Military Accuracy.

Welcome to book 01 of Pixies' Heroes (not really the series name).

I want to talk about why we might choose to forgo accuracy when it comes to military aspects in our stories, much like the classic TV show *Hogan's Heroes* (which was in my mind when I was working on the ideation of this series.)

As writers, we generally strive for accuracy in our depictions of history, culture, and military practices. Still, in the pursuit of a fun story, we sometimes need to take creative liberties. This is particularly true when it comes to comedy since the exaggeration and manipulation of reality is often what makes humor work.

Take *Hogan's Heroes* (https://en.wikipedia.org/wiki/Hogan's_Heroes TV show from 1965-1971), for example.

The show's depiction of a POW camp during World War II as a relaxed and comfortable place where American prisoners engage in all sorts of hijinks is far from the reality of the time. But, it's precisely this exaggeration and manipulation of reality that makes the show so enjoyable and memorable.

Similarly, in this urban fantasy stories, we chose to take creative liberties when it comes to the military aspects, such as depicting pixies as soldiers or having them engage in battles in fantastical ways and of course ALL the liberties with the military inaccuracies that are in this series (as opposed to *The Warrior series.*)

These exaggerations, I hope, add an element of humor and lightheartedness to these stories, making them more enjoyable for our readers. While accuracy is not always necessary, I believe it is important to respect the military and its practices.

Our exaggerations and manipulations are not intended to offend or belittle the real experiences of soldiers and their families.

As urban fantasy writers, we might choose to forgo accuracy when it comes to military aspects in our stories to pursue a good comedy and that's what we have chosen to do in this series.

To all of our military readers and others, I hope you enjoy the Pixies!

Ad Aeternitatem,

Michael Anderle

MORE STORIES with Michael newsletter HERE: https://michael.beehiiv.com/

GET SMOKED OR GO HOME

They say she's not good enough for the family business. Maybe it's because she was meant for something better.

Sometimes what looks like the worst day ever, is the beginning of our best adventure.

Idina takes that first step into a new life and gets the hell away from them to forge her own future.

But her calling is the one thing they are the most against. She joins the military just like Uncle Rick. The other family outcast.

A new Warrior is about to find out the true roots of the Moorfield name. Nothing will ever be the same.

<u>AVAILABLE ON AMAZON AND KINDLE UNLIMITED!</u>

BOOKS BY MARTHA CARR

THE LEIRA CHRONICLES
CASE FILES OF AN URBAN WITCH
THE EVERMORES CHRONICLES
CHRONICLES OF WINLAND UNDERWOOD
SOUL STONE MAGE
THE KACY CHRONICLES
MIDWEST MAGIC CHRONICLES
THE FAIRHAVEN CHRONICLES
DIARY OF A DARK MONSTER
I FEAR NO EVIL
THE DANIEL CODEX SERIES
SCHOOL OF NECESSARY MAGIC
SCHOOL OF NECESSARY MAGIC: RAINE CAMPBELL
ALISON BROWNSTONE
FEDERAL AGENTS OF MAGIC
SCIONS OF MAGIC
THE UNBELIEVABLE MR. BROWNSTONE
DWARF BOUNTY HUNTER
ACADEMY OF NECESSARY MAGIC
MAGIC CITY CHRONICLES
ROGUE AGENTS OF MAGIC
WITCH WARRIOR
THE AGENT OPERATIVE
BIG EASY BOUNTY HUNTER

[OTHER BOOKS BY JUDITH BERENS](#)

[OTHER BOOKS BY MARTHA CARR](#)

[**JOIN THE ORICERAN UNIVERSE FAN GROUP ON FACEBOOK!**](#)

BOOKS BY MICHAEL ANDERLE

Sign up for the LMBPN email list to be notified of new releases and special deals!

http://lmbpn.com/email/

For a complete list of books by Michael Anderle, please visit:

www.lmbpn.com/ma-books/

CONNECT WITH THE AUTHORS

Martha Carr Social
Website:
http://www.marthacarr.com
Facebook:
https://www.facebook.com/groups/MarthaCarrFans/

Michael Anderle

Website: http://lmbpn.com

Email List: https://michael.beehiiv.com/

https://www.facebook.com/LMBPNPublishing

https://twitter.com/MichaelAnderle

https://www.instagram.com/lmbpn_publishing/

https://www.bookbub.com/authors/michael-anderle

www.ingramcontent.com/pod-product-compliance
Lightning Source LLC
LaVergne TN
LVHW091718070526
838199LV00050B/2453